Weird Luck in the City of the Watcher

Volume One of the
City of the Watcher trilogy

Andrew M. Reichart

Weird Books for Weird People

Also by Andrew M. Reichart from Argawarga Press:

Wallflower Assassin

Time Traveling Blues in the City of the Watcher

Cannibal-King

City of the Watcher trilogy illustrated omnibus

Argawarga Press is an imprint of Autonomous Press that publishes strange fantasy, horror, and science fiction.

Autonomous Press is an independent publisher focusing on works about neurodivergence, queerness, and the various ways they can intersect with each other and with other aspects of identity and lived experience. We are a partnership including writers, poets, artists, musicians, community scholars, and professors. Each partner takes on a share of the work of managing the press and production, and all of our workers are co-owners.

Front Cover by Mike Bennewitz @sonofwitz

Interior by Casandra Johns

Originally published in 2012 by Argawarga Press

ISBN-13: 978-1-945955-33-4

Argawarga Press • argawarga.com

Contents

for Nick, Jeremy, & Brian

Prologue in Alexandria, New Jersey

Almost noon, New Year's Day, 1971. Aleck, thirteen, sat down on the top step to the basement and sighed in resignation, his breath trailing a long cloud out across the dead lawn. He watched Billy, below him, pound on the basement door again.

"Come on! Let us in already, you fascist pig!"

Aleck heard Damon shout something back through the door that sounded like *Buzz off, small fry.*

"It's my basement!" said Billy. "You don't even live here!"

"Forget about it," said Aleck. "The station's going to start playing it any minute."

"No way! What, we gonna listen to rock music upstairs with my hungover parents?"

"Ride our bikes back to my house."

"And listen on your dinky transistor radio?" Billy held up his fingers an inch apart. "And anyway, we'll miss the beginning!"

"They're playing the whole album, man. We won't miss much." Aleck got up. Looked across the dead lawn to his bike, lying on its side near the mailbox.

"No way. I am not going to submit to that imperialist pig-dog."

Aleck ignored this transparent attempt to sway him with revolutionary hyperbole. "If we leave right now, we might not miss anything."

"No way. I am not going to miss the opening of the new album from the best band in the universe, man." Billy turned to face the door. "We have a good hi-fi down here, and it's technically half mine, only half Grace's, and not Damon's at all."

"Property is theft, man," said Aleck, mostly to himself.

Billy banged on the door again. "Mom and Dad gave that hi-fi to both of us!" Damon said something back. Aleck heard other voices too, but couldn't distinguish them. Billy grumbled, spat, turned, and stomped back up the steps toward Aleck and ground level. "Come on, let's go under the porch."

"We can make it to my house it ten minutes on our bikes," said Aleck. Billy ignored him. Around the side of the house, they ducked behind the juniper bush, and slid into the cold, shadowy space under the porch: 'The Spider-Cave.' They crept across a cold floor of dusty dirt. Spiderwebs thickly laced the joists overhead.

"What the fuck was his reason this time?" asked Aleck.

"The usual. We're 'too young.'"

"Figures."

"They called us kids. 'Kids.' I'm thirteen!"

"Jerks."

They reached the dingy basement window and lay down on the ratty old cardboard air conditioner box. Billy's big sister Grace kept the basement room dimly lit, but the Spider-Cave was darker still even in daytime, so they could always see in without being seen. Grace had decorated her lair with oversized pillows and black light posters. Billy and his friends found themselves alter-nately welcomed and banned according to criteria that none of them could ever reliably discern.

"Where the hell is Mikey?" asked Billy.

Aleck shrugged. "He said he was coming."

"He's gonna miss it."

"So are we. We can't hear worth a dang down here, man. We shoulda gone to my house."

"If they turn it up loud enough."

"If you know the songs already," said Aleck. "But the first time, like we've never even heard it, man. Your brain can fill in the pieces but not if you never heard it."

"It's fine if they turn it up loud enough."

"It sounds like crap out here."

"Better than your transistor radio," said Billy.

Aleck pointed. "Damon's got a joint." Damon lit a hand-rolled cigarette with his Zippo lighter and passed it to Grace, who passed it to Damon's sidekick Luke, who passed it to Grace's friend Diane, who passed it to Diane's sister, Selene. "That's why they don't want us down there." Aleck found Grace's friends beautiful too, but none of them compared to her in his eyes; they never talked to him. Grace made him laugh out loud.

"That's bullshit," said Billy. "We've smoked pot with them a million times."

"You have, maybe," said Aleck. "I have maybe twice."

"Here," said a voice behind them.

Aleck jumped, banging his head on a joist. "Ow." He rubbed his skull. Spiderwebs had clotted in his shaggy hair. He turned and saw Mikey, offering a lit joint.

"Hey," said Billy in greeting. Then, "Hey!" He took the joint.

"I pilfered it from Grace's stash," said Mikey.

"Aw, man." Billy drew deeply. "You gotta stop doing that," he croaked.

"She'll never notice. Do you know how much pot she has in that old box? It's like they smoke a joint and then just keep rolling joints the whole time they're high. There must be twenty joints in there, plus a bag with enough grass in it for twenty more."

"I mean you gotta stop sneaking into my house," said Billy, still holding his breath. He passed the joint to Aleck, who hit it immediately.

"Your mom said something about dinner at seven," said Mikey. "She told me to tell you to make sure you're back in time from whatever it is we go do."

Billy exhaled in a gust, making a cloud of smoke and mist. "My *mom* saw you?"

"I saw her," said Mikey, "so I said hi."

"Did she see you go into Grace's room?"

"No, of course not."

"You shouldn't steal, though, man," said Aleck, "except from The Man. It's against our charter."

"I didn't steal it, man, I pilfered it. The Trespassers' Club Charter specifically says moderate pilfering is a-okay. If there was just five joints it woulda been stealing, and I wouldn't of done it. But one out of twenty is like nothing."

"Nice logic." Aleck exhaled. "You should work for Nixon."

Mikey smirked, unfazed by this most grave of insults. "Thanks, Che fuckin' Guevara."

Aleck took a second hit before passing the joint back. He wanted to debate the distinction between theft and pilfering, in the context of the principles of their agreed-upon number one heroes, the revolutionary anti-racist White Panther Party: "rock 'n roll, dope, sex in the streets, and the abolishing of capitalism," as Aleck had read in *Rolling Stone*. However, he just now found himself feeling very, very high. Did his double-hit count as pilfering, he wondered? The cramped space under the porch seemed frighteningly stifling. His thoughts spiraled from worry to worry: Grace catching them for stealing her grass. Damon catching them spying. Billy's mom catching them smoking under the porch. Billy and Mikey's conversation gradually threaded its way back into Aleck's attention: something about girls.

"Diane's foxy," said Mikey, "but nowhere near as foxy as Grace."

"Yeah but Grace is my sister," said Billy. "I'm not gonna make it with my own sister, man."

"Like you're gonna make it with Diane?" Mikey laughed.

"I can't hear anything," said Aleck. "Did it start yet?"

"No it didn't start yet." Billy passed the inch-long joint to

Aleck. Aleck, too high to remember he was already too high, took a drag and passed it to Mikey, feeling dizzy and wishing he'd left well enough alone.

"I can't believe they wouldn't let us in," said Mikey. "They're the ones who turned us on to Black Sabbath in the first place. It ain't right. They have, like, a responsibility." He hit the joint.

"Tell that to Damon," said Billy.

"Okay," croaked Mikey, holding his breath. "Hey Damon!" He reached to knock on the window. Billy slapped his hand away. The roach flew up into a spiderweb, hung there, burned itself free, and fell to the ground. Mikey broke into a fit of mixed coughing and laughing. Billy tried to cover Mikey's mouth. Aleck retrieved the roach from the dirt and took a hit off of it, remembering only as he did so that he'd perhaps best not. He broke into a coughing fit as well. Billy tried to cover Aleck's mouth while holding onto Mikey and poked Aleck in the eye. Aleck jumped and hit his head again.

"Shh!" Billy peered into the basement from the edge of the window. "Shh! Shh!" Aleck and Mikey stifled their coughing fits. Billy turned and gave them an ugly stare. "Man, keep it down!"

"We're not gonna be able to hear jack squat out here." Aleck spoke through his cough.

"Hey I know," said Mikey, also still coughing. "We should listen to it in Damon's car."

"You're addlebrained," said Billy. Aleck and Mikey stared at him, coughing and laughing. "My grandma says that. 'You're addlebrained.'"

"I reckon you hear that a lot from her," said Mikey. Painful laughter overtook Aleck. Mikey turned like a crab, still coughing, and began crawling back out of the Spider-Cave.

"Aw, man, where you going?"

"He's right," said Aleck, following. At the edge of the porch, Aleck watched Mikey poke his head out behind the juniper bush, look right and left, and slide out. Aleck followed. The instant they emerged they broke into an easy, casual stroll toward the corner of the house as if they'd been strolling all along, hands in the pockets of their heavy jackets. Billy scampered after them and then switched smoothly into a matching stride. They circled behind the house, arguing quietly.

"Look," said Billy. "No way."

"He'd let you," said Mikey. "Come on, man, he even let you drive the thing. You can listen to the radio once in a while."

"You want to ask his permission?" Billy pointed at the basement door. "Go ask him."

"Come on, we're the Trespassers' Club," said Aleck.

"It's not like we're going to demolish his car," said Mikey. "I double-decker-dog-pecker dare you."

Billy winced at the magic phrase. "Okay." He pondered for a short moment. "I can tell him, just, 'You wouldn't even let me into my own basement, jerkoff, all I did was sit in your car.'"

Around the front of the house sat Damon's '70 Camaro convertible, cream-colored with fat red stripes. Damon had bought it in springtime, failing to consider the New Jersey winter. "Putting the top up doesn't even make a difference," Grace had observed through chattering teeth back in mid-November.

"Sure it does," Damon had said. "It cuts the wind."

Over the past several weeks, as winter increased, Aleck heard Grace repeat her complaint many times, while he shivered in the back seat with Billy and Mikey. Damon soon stopped repeating his claim about the wind and just turned up the heater.

Mikey caressed the Camaro's sweet curves of cold metal. The doors were unlocked. Aleck got in back. Billy insisted on taking tho driver's seat. "Just in case you get crazy."

"Man, come on, the keys aren't even in the ignition." Mikey got in the passenger side. "Hold on, yes they are."

"Hands off." Billy shut his heavy steel door as quietly as he could. Mikey followed suit.

Billy turned on the radio and tuned the dial. The DJ announced that Black Sabbath's new album, *Paranoid*, would begin momentarily.

Mikey produced another joint. Billy scowled. "Okay, so I took two. Now she's down to eighteen. It's still just pilfering." He lit it with his infamous Zippo lighter.

Aleck shook his head. "Whoa, I do not need any more."

Mikey passed him the joint. "You're not going anywhere, man."

Aleck frowned and took a shallow hit. He sank into the back seat, holding the joint out to Billy.

It was cold in the car. Mikey reached over and turned on the ignition. Billy switched it off and looked around in a panic.

"He's not going to hear if you don't like rev it. We need the heater."

Billy clenched his jaw and gently turned the engine on again.

Black Sabbath's second album, *Paranoid*, played.

Aleck's thoughts swirled. He sank into weird depths. He saw battlefields, and madness, and the solar system, and then nothing but a sea of stars.

Eventually, somewhere, he heard a faint voice say, "I double-decker-dog-pecker dare you."

Aleck noticed the cold, and the wind. His eyes creaked open, and he saw light glaring down from a bright gray sky. The top was down. He felt no fear.

The radio blared over the noise of the freezing wind as skeletal trees flew past on either side. Billy downshifted into a turn, and then upshifted out of it. "I'm getting the hang of it," he shouted.

"Is it improving your handling like Damon said?" yelled Mikey.

Aleck feared nothing. Felt almost afraid of his lack of fear, but decided instead to sink back into the music and the seat. He watched the rapidly passing woods. The music transported him to another reality. "Rock and roll is going to save the world!" he roared.

As though in reply, the singer on the radio howled, "Yeah!"

"Yeah!" screamed the three of them.

"This is the best music ever made," said Billy.

"Watch this turn," said Mikey. "Remember this turn? 'The Doomer'?"

"What?" said Billy.

The convertible flew off the road.

•

Aleck felt dizzy. He couldn't find his coat. Shuddering in the cold, he walked among the trees, looking for the car. "How'd I get so sweaty?" he mumbled, wiping his eyes. His hands came away red. He walked faster then. Should he call for help? Through the trees he saw some sort of building. He tried to run, but his legs felt too heavy. Lurching forward, he pushed open the door—

•

Aleck floated in darkness, numb. He saw nothing but stars.

A voice spoke to him. "How did you come here?"

"Aw, man, am I dead?" He looked around but could see no one. "You're an angel, right?"

"How did you travel here?" asked the angel.

"We drove. I think Billy crashed the car."

"What? Say that again?"

"Where are Billy and Mikey?"

"You and I are the only ones here," said the angel. "My Master approaches."

"Your master? What, you mean Jesus?"

No reply. Aleck hung motionless in the dark. Where were Billy and Mikey? He felt empty and alone.

Prologue in the House of the Watcher

Apraxos the Watcher paced around his cold stone chamber, lighting candles, gritting his teeth. The nightmare still clung to him. He tried stomping himself awake, and vermin scampered at his approach. *The dream was just a dream*, he told himself. *Even if the Cannibal-King did come, my Astral Web would trap him.*

Running footsteps echoed down the hall outside the cham-ber, and a young Deep One burst in, short of breath. "Master, come quick!"

"What do you want!" snapped Apraxos from behind his white mask.

"Something's been caught in the Astral Web!"

That stunned him for a moment. Then he shouted "Co-inci-dence!" at the room, clenching his fists at his sides. "There is no 'Cannibal-King,' the Web has simply caught another unlucky world-jumper! Just another meal for the spirit-eaters!"

"Y-yes, my lord?"

He looked down at the Deep One. She cowered, which made him feel a little better. "I beg your pardon, my dear." He approached, demeanor suddenly gentle, attuning the subtle magics of his plain white mask to emanate calm rather than fearsomeness. "I did not mean to startle you. You simply in-terrupted my meditations; I beg your forgiveness for my temper."

He stood close, looming over her. Her dry skin had started to crack, and her gill-fronds drooped like wilted kelp: his minions clearly hadn't allowed her to immerse for several days.

"Of course, Master." She stared up at him.

Behind his mask, Apraxos smiled. "How long have you served us, down here in the House of the Watcher?" He rested his gnarled, gloved hand on her shoulder.

"A–a few days, Master. I am not sure." Her voice trembled as she looked around the stark stone bedchamber. "I know not how to mark time, here inside the Hollow World, with neither sun nor tide to judge by."

"And where did you come from, sweet fishling?" He touched her lank hair.

"I was...*brought*...from Pesk-Orn Bay several weeks ago. I served in the University until your man Blue Thresner selected me to serve here."

"How interesting." Apraxos smiled down at her. "Do you know why I ask these things of you...what was your name?"

"Thralela."

"Thralela, do you know why I seek to know you personally?"

"No, Master...."

"Because I want you to trust me, my dear. I want you to feel safe here — to know that I am a kind master, and a devoted protector." He caressed her cheek. "Do you know why this is so important to me?"

"No, Master...."

He grabbed her by the neck and lifted her off the ground. He held her face up to his blank mask, projecting menace out through the eyeholes and into her eyes. "Because the shock of betrayal at the time of death will make your soul taste all the sweeter." He crushed her throat in his gloved fist, pressing his mask against her face and whispering her name: "Thralela, Thralela, Thralela." Her soul wafted out of her mouth and in through the mask's narrow nostrils. It burned inside Apraxos, surging into his heart and limbs.

He tossed the corpse aside and swept confidently out of his chamber, buoyed upon Thralela's life-force. "Coincidence," he said again as he strode down the hall. "Nothing to worry about, I'm sure." But the aetheric flame of Thralela's soul burned down to an ectoplasmic cinder, then spirit-ash, then nothingness. Nervousness crept swiftly back into his stomach, and he started gritting his teeth again. Behind him, the vermin scampered over one another to reach Thralela's corpse.

•

Apraxos stepped out atop the Tower of the Skull. Overhead, clouds hid the interior of the Hollow World. Dark, bleak landscape surrounded his castle on three sides; ahead, the vista overlooked the yawning mouth of a wide black pit. A bottomless pit, leading to the surface world. In the center of the Tower's roof squatted a pedestal, upon which sat a gleaming skull of gold: the Skull of Kaios. Beside the pedestal knelt a man-shaped figure, its body made of articulated metal and its head made of glass, peering into the Skull's eye sockets.

"Thresner," said Apraxos.

With a series of little clangs the metal man snapped awk-wardly to his feet. "Minister Apraxos!" Blue Thresner's voice resonated from a hole in his chest. Within the glass sphere, in a murky liquid, floated the severed head of a very old Shallow One. The eyes gaped open and swiveled in their sockets, but his lips, crudely sewn shut, did not move as he spoke. "The Astral Web has caught an interloper," came his metallic voice. He gestured to the golden Skull on the pedestal. "His astral body floats within."

"Who is it?" asked Apraxos, failing to conceal his impatience.

"I do not know." Thresner's voice sounded hollow. "He seems agitated."

"You have been able to communicate with him, then?"

"Yes, Minister. Although he speaks oddly."

"You have cast spells to determine his intended destination and mode of travel?"

"Yes, Minister. He came here through a gate; if your Web had not caught him, he would have emerged in the Village of Corpse-water, in the middle of Bitchwood."

"Corpsewater." Apraxos hissed almost inaudibly.

"Yes, Minister. However, this traveler expressed no awareness of having passed through a gate, nor any recognition of the astral world-between-worlds, nor any knowledge of Corpsewater."

Apraxos breathed a heavy sigh. "Just another accidental, then."

"Yes, my lord. Another Earthling, in this case."

"Another?"

"Yes, Minister."

Apraxos sighed with relief once more. The Cannibal-King and his Heralds could never originate on a low-magic world like Earth. "Another snack for the spirit-eaters, then. Well, let's have some sport first, shall we?"

"Oh yes, Minister Apraxos." Thresner twisted his stitched mouth into something like a smile.

Apraxos snatched up the Skull of Kaios and stared into its eye sockets. "Earthling!" he called loudly, conveying his voice into the Astral Web. "Can you hear me?"

A young man's voice came from within the hollow Skull. "Man, where the hell am I? Where are my friends?"

"We are your friends. Tell me what you see, boy."

"Stars," came the voice from the Skull. "I can't feel anything. Where are Billy and Mikey? Am I dead?"

"You are simply in the astral plane." Apraxos maintained a reassuring tone. "I do not think you are dead."

"I'm on a *plane?*" The voice sounded baffled and afraid. "We were in a car crash, not a plane. Damon's gonna frickin' kill us...."

"I know of nowhere called *Akarkrash*." Apraxos furrowed his brow behind his mask. "But I do not think you are at risk from any demons. Consider me your friend and ally; my name is Minister Apraxos, and I will do all I can to assist and protect you. Do not worry."

"What the hell is going on? Where am I?"

"Tell me what you remember." Apraxos spoke slowly into the Skull, trying to remain patient.

"We were listening to the new Black Sabbath album in Damon's car, and we kinda decided to go for a ride. But it's not like we *stole* it, man, he let us drive it before."

"I do not understand."

"Black frickin' Sabbath, man! What, do you live in a hole in the ground?"

Apraxos scowled at this unwittingly accurate turn of phrase. "Please, explain."

The young man sang in an exaggerated twang: "*'Casting his shadow, weaving his spell, funny clothes, tinkling bell....*' You know? That goosestepper Damon wouldn't let us hang with them in the basement. So we listened to it in his Camaro instead. You gotta hear the new record, man, holy shit."

"Your clarification obfuscates." Apraxos felt his patience beginning to erode.

"Look, we just kinda decided to go for a ride, man, I don't know how it happened. I know it was a stupid idea. Christ, I may as well be dead, I think we probably totaled Damon's car."

Apraxos looked at Thresner.

Thresner shrugged with a sound of metal grating upon metal. "I understand he wished to attend a hanging in a basement, but aside from that, I fear I apprehend little."

"Send the spirit-eaters." Apraxos turned to leave.

"A bit longer, my lord. We may learn something interesting yet."

"He speaks entirely in gibberish," said Apraxos, but he turned back to the Skull. "Tell me what happened next." He made no attempt to hide the irked resignation in his voice.

"I don't know, man. I can't feel anything. This is freaking me out, aren't you freaked out? Where are you? I think I went through the windshield.... I must be dead, or in a coma or something. I remember walking through Bitchwood, trying to find my way back to the car...."

That startled Apraxos. "Bitchwood?"

"Oh uh Birch Wood, ha ha, we call it Bitch Wood and a couple years ago we changed the — I mean, somebody changed the sign to say Bitch Wood, I don't know who did it."

"He has a Bitchwood in his world!" said Thresner.

"Yes. Such parallels are to be expected, in the vicinity of a gate between two worlds." Apraxos turned again to the Skull. "My friend, you are simply in the astral plane. I do not understand why you repeatedly speculate that you have died."

"Dude, are you burnt out from too much acid or something? Billy drove Damon's car into a ditch at seventy frickin' million miles an hour, I went face-first through the windshield, last I remember I was covered in blood, now I can't feel my body and all I can see anywhere is stars floating all around me!"

"Ah," said Thresner, "I believe his agitation stems from some sort of injury."

"Indeed," said Apraxos. "You see? It must be an instance of 'weird luck.' Consider: accidentally passing through a gate to Corpsewater, immediately after becoming seriously injured? Supremely improbable."

"Corpsewater's magic healing pool!"

"Exactly."

"Hey," came the small voice from inside the golden Skull. "Dude, you there?"

Thresner laughed hollowly. "Unfortunately for him, your Astral Web has interrupted his extraordinary luck."

"Quite." Apraxos chuckled. "Because 'weird' does not always mean 'good,' my dear Thresner."

The voice in the Skull spoke again. "Look, I'm sorry I called you an acid burnout."

Apraxos set the Skull back down on the pedestal. "Well, Thresner, this has been entertaining, but my curiosity is satisfied. Fetch the spirit-eaters."

"Very well, my lord." Thresner opened a compartment in the pedestal and brought out a small, ornately carved wooden box.

"Hey, man, where are you?" came the voice from within the Skull.

"Patience, my friend. Don't go anywhere." Apraxos laughed at his own joke.

"Something's coming, man."

"I beg your pardon?" Apraxos squinted into the Skull's eye sockets.

"It sounds like a frickin' truck or something. Holy shit!"

Blinding light flashed out from the Skull, and an explosion knocked Apraxos and Thresner sprawling.

•

Apraxos found himself lying flat on his back. His ears rang. Aching, he struggled to his feet. On the far side of the pedestal Thresner lay in a puddle, his glass helm smashed, his withered head trailing braided cords into the neck-hole. "Minister, help," croaked the speaker-hole in his chest. The spirit-eater box lay broken and empty beside him.

Half of the Skull of Kaios, the face, lay beside the pedestal, looking up at Apraxos. He saw the other half, the cranium, glittering on the far side of the tower roof.

Apraxos stooped and picked up the front half of the Skull, and could sense at a touch that his Astral Web had been destroyed.

He recalled a stanza from the *Book of the Cannibal-King*, one of the ancient prophecies Great Kaios himself had carved onto his stone pillars. A passage that Apraxos, in his redaction centuries ago, had chiseled away into stone chips and dust:

> *Nor at first will the Herald be known by his face,*
> *Though his face bear the scars of strange fortune;*
> *And Akaz preserves the Herald's portion*
> *Of luck till the end of the chase.*
> *The Herald speaks now of unknowable things,*
> *To mark the arrival of Cannibal-King.*

Apraxos stood for a long while, not moving, pondering that passage.

"Minister...." Thresner groaned from the hole in his chest.

"I will send someone to aid you." Apraxos let the piece of Skull drop from his hand. "I must go to Corpsewater."

He walked down the long spiral stairway.

The First
Herald

WEIRD LUCK (*slang*): see CHRONIC SYNCHRO-
NICITY SYNDROME, EXTREME (or ECSS)

see also CHRONIC SYNCHRONICITY SYNDROME,
COMMON (or CCSS)

see also CIRCLES; DESTINY; FATE; KENOSHA;
LATTICE OF COINCIDENCE; LUCK PLANE; PER-
FECT SYNCHRO; SIMULTANEITY; SPIN; SPIRAL
ARRAY; SYNCHRONICITY; WHEELS

— from *A Layman's Interdimensional Encyclopedia*,
by Prof. Xenion D. Clark, O.8.D.

·

A distant rumble grabbed Aleck's attention. He spotted a dark shape moving behind the stars. "Something's coming, man!" he said to the pair of invisible, goofy angels. A roar and a rattling accompanied the approaching shadow, like the sound of a big, old truck. The shadow grew suddenly huge, and lightning flashed from star to star—

Aleck fell, very slowly, through darkness. He could see no more stars, only a pale gray light that coruscated through rippling shadows of smoky black. Silence.

A white Ford cargo van floated noisily past. Aleck's eyes met with the driver's for a flash — a red-haired woman — and the van disappeared.

What the—?

Then Aleck stumbled out into daylight.

Standing on unsteady legs, he dazedly looked over his surroundings. People, naked, unlike any he'd seen before, sat on boulders around a steaming pool. Gnarled trees and shaggy hedges screened the pool from whatever lay beyond.

"I'm alive!" he tried to say; but the words came out more like *ai walai.* Moving his mouth sent a wave of agony across his face. He staggered from the pain, tripped, and sprawled headlong into the pool.

Hands dragged him down into the hot water. Opening his eyes, he found himself face to face with a grinning skull: a bone-faced mermaid held him by the shirt. He struggled to free himself from her grip. His blood-soaked t-shirt released a pale red cloud into the water.

"Calm yourself." The mermaid lashed her eel-like tail around Aleck's thighs.

A wave of euphoria passed up his spine, and Aleck felt calm despite himself. He stared into the glistening black spheres that swirled in the mermaid's bony eye sockets. He serenely breathed the hot water of the pool, in and out, in and out. *This is one of those deadly hallucinations they talk about in anti-drug assemblies at school,* he thought. Still, his calm didn't waver. *Well,* he thought, *if this is drowning, it's not so bad.*

"Poor boy." The mermaid ran her fingers across his face. Aleck felt her pressing his lower lip back together, massaging the deep gashes across his brow and jaw. He felt no pain at her touch.

"There, all better." *How can I hear her speaking underwater?* he thought. "Up you go."

"No, wait, who are you?" Aleck's voice traveled through water as though it were air. She shoved him up to the surface without replying. Various hands grabbed him from above and hauled him up onto a shady rock.

Whoever pulled him up, Aleck found himself instead face to face with an enormous black wolf. The huge beast stared at him with flaming embers for eyes. Aleck froze, though he still felt mostly calm from whatever the mermaid had done to him. He stared back.

The wolf turned and leaned over the pool. Opening its jaws, it coughed, coughed again, and retched. Then it vomited out into the pool a limp and bloodied man-shaped figure, long-limbed and indeed, impossibly, fully the size of the wolf itself. A pair of blue hands pulled the body down. The wolf looked at Aleck with flickering eyes, cocked its head, and strolled away.

Aleck looked around. The short, wiry-limbed, pot-bellied people around the pool smiled at him. He pointed after the wolf. Some smiled, some shrugged, some ignored him. One person made a funny snarling sound. Someone laughed, and someone else shushed them.

Beside the pool stood a large, wooden building. A door hung open, revealing what looked like an old-fashioned kitchen. *The door I must've come through*, Aleck thought; then, *wait, what am I thinking?* Everyone's shoes and clothes lay neatly piled near the door.

Someone burst up from the water, landed in a crouch, and leapt to their feet.

Aleck yelled in surprise.

A man loomed overhead, at least seven feet tall. Though no longer covered in blood, Aleck easily recognized the figure the wolf had just spat into the pool. A trick of the tree-shade mottled his skin in gray and turned his hair greenish. He worked his shoulder in a circle as though loosening a sore muscle. "Greetings, O First Herald," he said in a deep, resonant voice. He bowed to Aleck reverently. "We honor your arrival." He crouched, and full sunlight fell upon him through a break in the trees. He had, in fact, gray skin covered in black spiral tattoos; no trick of the light at all. Matted green braids dangled across his shoulders. "Welcome to Corpsewater, Young Aleck. It is a great honor that your arrival should occur in our village." He smiled, baring wolf-like fangs. "Hungry?"

Aleck looked around. "Where are my friends?"

"We're your friends," said the tall man.

"You too, huh?" asked Aleck.

The small people smiled at him, and several of them waved in greeting. "Eat something, boy," said an old woman. Someone laughed.

"I mean, where are Billy and Mikey?"

"Maybe he wants a smoke first," said a man with a scraggly black beard. More laughter.

The fanged, green-haired man-creature raised his eyebrows. "Smoke?"

"I don't smoke."

The fanged man sniffed the front of Aleck's shirt and gave him a sidewise look. Everyone laughed at that.

"Well I mean I was just smoking a little with my friends, but not cigarettes. I mean, just cigarettes. You haven't seen Billy and Mikey?" *How can he smell that on my doused shirt, anyway?*

"No one came through the door but you."

Aleck stared into space. *Is this real?*

The fanged man offered Aleck his hand. "I'm the Cook." Then he pulled his hand back slightly. "Do you do the Clasp where you come from?"

"Uh, yeah." Aleck reached forth. The Cook's grip felt solid as a tree-bole yet surprisingly gentle. "How in heck do you know my name?"

"Cook has visions," said the old woman.

"Hungry?" repeated the Cook.

Aleck put a hand to his face. Deep grooves crossed the left half, from jaw to hairline, nose to ear. He could feel the gap in his eyebrow, and the tiny cleft in each lip. Nothing hurt. He felt great — healthy, awake, and clear-headed. Yet a minute ago, simply moving his mouth to speak had hurt enough to make him faint. He glanced down at the pool, his freshly-scarred reflection wavering on the rippled surface. He no longer felt wasted from smoking weed with his friends; his mind, despite the impossible stimuli surrounding him, felt calm and clear. Crystal-clear sober through and through.

"This is real?" He looked up. Everyone laughed heartily at that.

"This is the village of Corpsewater," said the Cook, "on the Isle of Kaios. Both very real. Your face has just been healed by the Corpsewater Nymph. She has magic powers." He cocked his head and asked, in a humorous tone, "Aren't there magic powers where you come from?" More laughter.

Aleck considered, wondering if this question proved he was dreaming. "No," he said. "No magic."

The assembly fell quiet.

The Cook lunged his face near Aleck's and sniffed. "Nonsense," he laughed, settling back down on his haunches. "You are the First Herald. I can smell it. Magic lays thick upon you."

Aleck pressed his hands against the surface of the boulder beneath him. Its smooth, hard surface couldn't feel more real. If this was a dream, it was unlike any dream he'd had yet. He looked around at the smiling faces of the people lounging around the pool. They looked human, but he couldn't place them from any folk he'd ever seen — not in New Jersey, nor on television, nor in *National Geographic*.

"Make him some porridge, Cook," said someone.

"No, give him the stew."

"What about some of them birds you shot?"

The stillness broke as everyone offered their suggestions for Aleck's meal. They spoke English. Their accent didn't sound like any he'd ever heard.

"Here's the Ostler," said the Cook.

Out from the kitchen came a man with a big pot-belly, wearing tall, polished boots of brown leather and a conical hat with gaudy feathers. Over his plain shirt and breeches he wore a long, embroidered vest. The conversation about food continued without interruption around them.

"Oho," said the Ostler. "Here he is! First Herald of the Cannibal-King, is it? As you predicted, Cook?"

"Aye."

"What?" asked Aleck.

"Welcome to Corpsewater." The Ostler sat down beside them and shook Aleck's hand. "I'm the Ostler of our Inn," gesturing to the building. "Which makes me more or less Mayor of our fine village, what with our real Mayor lost up on Zan-Zerkin's Ridge."

"So you aren't some nudist colony," asked Aleck.

"Now, I'm not sure I could say for sure one way or the other," replied the Ostler. "Have you had anything to eat?"

"Not just yet."

"I see you've been in the pool." He tugged at Aleck's wet sleeve between thumb and forefinger. Furrowed his shaggy brows. "Customarily, we disrobe first. Are you shy?"

Aleck decided he couldn't possibly be asleep. Way too much weird-ass detail that he never would have come up with on his own. Which meant only one thing.

"We're not on Earth, are we."

"I'm on earth." The Ostler sincerely patted the patch of

dirt he sat upon. "You and Cook are on a rock."

The Cook laughed. "'Earth' is what he calls his home world, Ostler."

"Oh." The Ostler took off his feathered hat and ran his fingers across his thinly-haired pate. "You know I don't have much of a knack for those metaphysics, Cook. I'm a practical man."

"Get the boy some dry clothes," said the old woman.

The Cook stood up and pulled on a pair of tattered rawhide pants. "I'll heat up some of that stew." He ambled into the kitchen.

"Well," said the Ostler, "welcome to Corpsewater, young Herald of Earth. I daresay you'll like it in our village. We all do."

"Why the heck do you guys speak English?"

"What is *glish*?"

"What?"

"You said we speak in *glish*."

"Uh, never mind."

•

Aleck did his best to resign himself to the thought that, for now at least, Billy and Mikey were nowhere to be found and he couldn't do a thing about it. Knowing them, they were safe back on Earth, and not even hurt like he himself had been. But their absence gnawed at him.

He and the Ostler sat and ate with the villagers at long, tree-shaded tables on the Inn's front lawn. A skull carved in bas-relief on the main lintel represented the Inn's name, which the Ostler had proudly proclaimed as *The Sign of Death's Door*. The village of Corpsewater lay strewn about them on the small hill: huts, cabins, and small livestock pens surrounded by a palisade of sharpened logs. Outside the palisade lay a few fields and groves. Past the cultivated land, hilly forest rolled away and up. A mountain dominated the horizon, crowned askew by the setting sun. Wild magenta sunset arced beyond.

The people from the pool sat around them, dressed in browns and greens with red and yellow accents. Their old, patched clothing looked sturdy and comfortable. As Aleck and the Ostler ate, more Corpsewater folk joined them — old folks, scampering children, men and women of all ages and sizes — until it seemed the whole village must have arrived. Aleck noticed that many people carried beautifully carved walking sticks, decorated with bands of copper and large inset stones.

"Look, Mister Ostler, this is kind of freaking me out. Okay, I'm on another world, I can dig that. No idea how I got here, but here I am. Not just any world, though, a magic world. Okay, I can accept that too, I mean magic obviously got me here, plus it fixed my face so I'm not entirely complaining. But the Cook has some freaking *prophecy* about me, *specifically*?"

"Ah," said the Ostler. "I was just getting to that. Now, our clans, Corpsewater and elsewhere, are called Digglies, because we till the earth. The Cook is of another sort: his folk are forest people. We call them the Wilders; you can guess why." He handed Aleck an ornate earthenware platter with several small, roasted fowl on it. Aleck resigned himself to the Ostler's mode of exegesis. "A lot of Wilders just go for raw meat, but the Cook is a staunch advocate of the art of cuisine. Here, try this on it," handing Aleck a glass cup of thin brown sauce with herbs floating on top. "Cooked or raw, the Wilders know some powerful magics. They are close friends with Akaz the God-Dog, and some of them are hundreds, maybe thousands of years old."

"How old is the Cook?"

The Ostler shrugged. "How old is a tree? How old is a rock? Who knows. Here, try this." He offered Aleck something that looked like squash and onions, marinated and baked. "The Cook has magic ways, that's what I'm trying to tell you, not how tall he is or how many fingers he has. He with his ancient mind can see things, and he has a divination-bone, one of the Shinbones of Kaios in fact, threaded with beads carved from the fangs of dead Wilders. It makes a fine rattle, and with it he talks to spirits and sees the future. He told us the First Herald was coming, just like in the prophecies of Kaios." He smiled and shrugged. "We like strangers, so we were waiting for you. Here." He handed Aleck a ceramic plate of steamed greens.

The Cook sat down beside Aleck, eating a small roast bird, bones and all. "Fresh volunteers in the kitchen," mouth full, chewing and crunching. "I eat now."

"Many thanks to you as always for your cooking, Cook. I was just telling young Aleck here about your Sacred Bone."

"Cook, how old are you?"

The Cook crunched and crunched and swallowed. Looked up for a long moment as though counting in his head. "Thirty-seven."

Aleck frowned at the Ostler.

The Ostler shrugged: "How old is a thirty-seven year old tree?"

Aleck stared into space for a second, then turned back to the Cook. "So how did you predict I was coming here?"

"I simply saw it in a rattle trance." He looked intently at his roast bird and took another bite. Something about his manner made Aleck wonder if he were telling the whole truth.

"What did you see? What's this 'First Herald' business?"

The Cook looked skyward. "In my vision I saw you wandering, bloody, in the woods." He glanced at Aleck. "I saw you stumble out through our kitchen door, just as you must have not long before we met. I sensed you were from another world. I know of such visitors, though I've never before met any. Minister Apraxos catches most of them."

That rang a bell. "Minister who?"

"Minister Apraxos," said the Cook. "Also called the Watcher."

"Shh," whispered the Ostler. "He is Listener as well as Watcher! He hears when his name is spoken!"

"That's a myth," said the Cook.

"I daresay not!" countered the Ostler.

"That's the guy I talked to," said Aleck.

"What?" exclaimed both Cook and Ostler.

"On my way here, I was in this place that was all stars, and that guy spoke to me, Minister Whatshisname. Minister Ass-Prick-Sauce."

The Cook nodded. "He trapped you in his Web, in the astral plane."

"He did say something about a plane. Though I still don't get what that had to do with it. I didn't see any plane. Just a big white van showed up just before I got away."

"You *escaped* from the Weird Minister?" The Ostler spoke louder than he intended. Conversations stopped and faces turned toward them.

"What did he say to you?" The Cook made no effort to keep their conversation secret.

"He said he was my friend."

The crowd stirred, and Aleck noticed for the first time that their ornamented walking sticks somewhat resembled clubs. Some, axes. And some of the Digglies ate with long copper knives. They regarded Aleck with grave faces.

Aleck braced himself to bolt. "Uh, I'm not his friend. I thought he was a jerkoff."

The Cook spoke to the crowd. "Be still. He is no friend to Apraxos. He has come to help the Master Summoner bring us the Cannibal-King."

"How do we know?" asked a big, gruff Diggly. "The Watcher already has a false Cannibal-King in General Goromath. Why not a False Herald to go with him? Sent here to trick us."

"You're making no sense," said the Ostler. "The Herald come *after* the King? If he comes after, he's not heralding anything." Some of the Digglies laughed. Others frowned.

"Wrong, Ostler," said the gruff Diggly. "The Watcher was apprentice of Oggo and Hoggo, whose magic twists everything. His False Herald would surely come after his False King."

"Preposterous," said the Ostler.

A rumbling, gravelly voice cut through the evening air. "He's right, Ostler." The fire-eyed wolf looked much bigger now, bigger than any dog, nearly the size of a moose unless Aleck was seeing things, which he might be. "About the magic of Oggo and Hoggo, anyways. Paradoxes like that are typical." The wolf's deep voice sounded like a mound of hot coals stirred with a shovel; his breath smelled like hot ashes and burned meat. His accent sounded like Aleck's. Earth. New Jersey, even. "But this is the real First Herald, no doubt about it." The wolf looked at Aleck. "Aleck, right?"

"What the freak...?"

"He has the sunburst scars, as foretold by Kaios," said the old woman.

The Cook stood, grinning at the wolf. "Greetings, Great Akaz." He bowed deeply.

"What in heck are you?" Aleck asked the wolf.

Akaz shrugged, the human gesture eerie in an animal body. "Giant talking fire-breathing wolf."

"You speak English."

"Yeah, lived on Earth awhile."

"But everyone else here speaks English, too."

"Yeah," said Akaz, "long story."

"What brings you to our fair village today, O Akaz?" The Ostler spoke nervously.

"Aside from dumping your wounded Cook into the pool, you mean?" asked Akaz. "I smelled food."

"You haven't come to eat the Herald?" spluttered the Ostler, jumping to his feet.

Akaz's laugh sounded like a giant prodding a pile of burning trees. "Not today. So what brings you to this fair village, kid?"

"I have no clue. One minute I was in New Jersey with Billy and Mikey—"

"Yeah, Doomer and whatshisname," interrupted Akaz.

"What?"

"Never mind, don't worry. Your friends are fine."

"How the heck do you know?"

"Trust me, I'm a magic wolf."

Aleck glowered at him.

"Look, just trust me for now. They survived the car crash. I can't say more, for a very goddamn good reason. Just roll with it. You were saying: one minute you're in Jersey."

Aleck frowned at him. "We're coming back to this."

"Sure, sure, later. So you're in Jersey."

Aleck took a deep breath. "Then I was floating in space and couldn't move, then there was a kaboom and I fell out through the kitchen door." He gestured at the Inn.

"A 'kaboom'."

"Yeah." Aleck shrugged. "At first it sounded like a truck, then there was thunder and lightning."

"A truck."

"Not like an eighteen-wheeler or anything. Like a delivery van."

"The Cannibal-King's van!" said Akaz. "Did you hear his wife's motorcycle?"

"What?" This was not the response Aleck expected to his tale of a van driving through outer space.

"Was there a motorcycle with the van!"

"I didn't see any motorcycle!"

"Hmm," growled Akaz.

"Maybe it was on the far side of the van when they passed me," joked Aleck.

Akaz nodded. "Could be."

That nod served as a last straw. "This is ridiculous! What the hell is going on here?" He looked from wolf to Cook to Ostler to Digglies.

"The Cannibal-King is coming to take down Apraxos the Watcher and his General Goromath," said the Cook. "You are one of the Cannibal-King's Heralds. Your appearance here marks his immanent arrival."

"What? Why me?"

"Look, kid," said Akaz, "story goes, you're destined to help save a little corner of this world from an awful dictatorship. Kaios foretold it a few hundred years ago. Whether or not it's fact, the people believe it, and I'm tellin' ya, just roll with it."

"Uh, okay, that sounds completely bananas."

"C'mon. It'll be fun." Akaz started up the inn's front steps.

The Cook, then, transformed into a huge, black crow and flapped away into the building, croaking loudly.

Aleck stared in the open doorway. Akaz loped through. Beyond the huge wolf, the swooping crow flashed into view for a moment. The Cook definitely no longer occupied the empty stretch of bench beside Aleck. The Cook really turned into a crow and flew away. Deep inside Aleck something shifted. A small, subtle increase in his capacity to accept his impossible circumstances, inspired by the graceful flight of the shapeshifting Cook, nudged him up past some sort of threshold. Equanimity washed through him. Somehow nothing about this world seemed weird.

"C'mon," said Akaz over his shoulder.

"No fuckin' way, man, till you answer a few questions."

Akaz looked back at Aleck. "You mean like how a giant talking fire breathing wolf on another world speaks English with a twentieth century American accent."

"No," said Aleck, "I don't give a fuck about that. I mean like what are your fucking politics, man."

The flames in Akaz's mouth roared in the wind of his laugh. "Seriously?" He turned around.

"Dead serious, before I call you comrade."

Akaz laughed again. "'Destroy a dictatorship' ain't enough for you?"

Aleck squinted at him. "How's your 'Cannibal-King' anything but a replacement dictator?"

"Eh, he's no king. It's just poetic. Like Run-DMC are the Kings of Rock."

"I don't know what that means. You're saying he doesn't take power."

"Supposedly," said Akaz, "he ends up making it impossible for anyone to take power, himself or otherwise."

"Hmm," said Aleck. "Ok." He got to his feet.

The Nymph of the Shrine

Aleck stood in the kitchen, looking out at the steaming pool. Akaz, beside him, had shrunk to the size of a Great Dane. "Shut the door."

Aleck did so. The kitchen door had no hinges, *how—?*

"When you're outside, in either location, the door opens into the respective local kitchen. But from inside the kitchen—"

"I have no idea what you're talking about," said Aleck.

"Shut up and listen. Push on the left side, and it opens back out to the pool in Corpsewater. Push on the right side and it opens onto the yard behind the *God-Dog*."

"The what?"

"*The Sign of the God-Dog.* My bar back in the city."

"Your bar," said Aleck, bewildered.

"Technically it's an inn, I reckon. There's rooms for rent, that makes it an inn. It'll be the safest place for you to stay in Melkhaios, assuming we get any nap time at all in the next few days."

"I don't get why the door doesn't just fall out of the door-way," said Aleck. "There's no hinges."

"Aleck."

"Yeah?"

"It's a magic door."

"Oh."

"Let's go."

"Where do I push to get back to New Jersey?"

"Nowhere," said Akaz.

"How did I get here through this door, then?"

"That was a fluke. Momentary link from my bar to New Jersey. Then you stumbled from my bar to here. Happens. Link's gone now, but suffice it to say that we can find you a different way back. I'll explain later."

"How the hell are we gonna do that?"

"Later, dammit."

Aleck sighed and looked at the door. Centuries of daily use had worn their way into the surface of the left side. Aleck pushed tentatively on the unmarred right side, and the door opened outward. Beyond lay dirt for a few yards, then grass, then trees. He walked through.

Dizziness and nausea overtook him, and he stumbled headlong down a short flight of steps to sprawl face-first on dusty ground. He lay there a moment, head spinning. A large crow flew out through the door.

Akaz sniffed at Aleck. "You okay?"

"I think so," muttered Aleck, not moving.

The crow wheeled around and landed beside Aleck. "Feel dizzy?" it asked, in the Cook's voice.

Aleck lifted his head to look at them. "Uh-huh."

"Gonna puke?" asked Akaz.

The thought hadn't occurred to him, but Aleck's stomach lurched at the suggestion. Clenching his eyes and mouth shut, he swallowed spit and took a deep breath. "No."

"Some folks don't take well to teleportation," said Akaz.

Aleck couldn't recall feeling nauseated when he arrived in Corpsewater. Then again, he'd had more significant discomforts at the time. "I guess I'm one of those people."

"Good to know. We can maybe try to avoid it. Come on, let's go up on the roof so I can show you some landmarks."

Aleck got to his feet and took several deep breaths, taking in his first sight of the *God-Dog*. It was the most eccentric building he had ever set eyes on. An old, gangling stone tower loomed over a three-story assemblage of mismatched gables, balconies, and protruding dormer windows. Lawns and dusty paths surrounded it; beyond them, nothing but trees. "We're in the city?"

"Come up to the roof," said Akaz. "You'll see."

●

The Cook stood naked, inhumanly tall and thin, one foot on the low parapet. Late sunlight glowed upon his gray skin, the spirally black tattoos, his leaf-green braids. He turned into a crow again. The black bird hopped along the edge of the roof.

Aleck and Akaz stood on the stone tower's flat roof, looking out upon the hilly city. A wooded mountain towered over the landscape. The sky grew slowly darker behind it. From the mountain's foot, a river threaded down between old, ornate buildings and under bridges of pale stone. Long shadows stretched across streets and plazas. The river emptied into a bay ringed by distant black hills; across the bay, a red sun leaned toward the horizon among purple clouds shaped like chaos. Directly below the sun, far in the distance, rose a strange, tiny spire. The bay water glittered with golden light.

Aleck looked around. Though most buildings stood intact, much of the sprawling city looked ruined. Empty lots lay strewn with stones of structures fallen long ago. Many buildings seemed to have been rebuilt out of rubble, some crudely, some craftily. Outside the city, a forest blanketed the hills to the horizon. The woods cast a spur here into the neighborhood of the *God-Dog*, surrounding it with tall trees.

"Corpsewater is back on the other side of Mount Kaios," said Akaz. "You musta seen the mountain from the other direction when you were there. From this side you can see the Great Stone Face, though. See?"

Aleck squinted, trying to make out details. "What face? — *Oh my god.*"

On the side of the mountain, half the height of the mountain, loomed a titanic, brooding face of carved stone overgrown with trees.

"That's Kaios the Summoner, founder of the city of Melkhaios."

"Is he the 'Master Summoner'? The one I'm supposedly helping to summon the Cannibal-King?"

"Not really," said Akaz. "It's complicated. I mean, no, Kaios died long ago."

"He doesn't look happy."

"He left that face behind when he died. He and his mountain-spirit allies carved it the night before."

"Like, grim, even."

"Yeah, you could say they didn't especially care for the way the city turned out."

"How do you mean?"

"Melkhaios started out as a sort of utopian artists' colony. But it was overrun by Normals."

"Oh." Aleck wondered what it meant to be overrun by Normals.

"The Normals are worse than the Herax, if you ask me," said Akaz.

"What's the Herax?" Aleck felt saturated with new weird names.

"General Goromath's army. See that big wall to the east?"

"Which way's east?"

"Away from the sunset, goofus. At the foot of the mountain."

"Oh, yeah. Well, you know, I thought East might be different on this planet or something." Aleck hadn't thought anything of the sort, and sounded unconvincing even to himself.

A gigantic wall of stacked rubble dominated the eastern end of the city. "That's the Zone of the Herax," said Akaz. "They conquered Melkhaios after the Normals did, after Kaios died."

"They're General Who's army?"

"General Goromath."

"So who is he?"

"The False Cannibal-King. Mass-murdering dictator. That guy you met in the astral plane, Minister Apraxos, 'the Watcher, ' is officially just Goromath's court sorceror. But in reality, the Watcher pulls the strings. Co-opting the old prophecies of Kaios, that's his scheme. He also twisted the old Circus—"

"'Circus'?"

"See that stadium, left of the Herax Zone?" Akaz pointed with his snout. Aleck saw what looked like a large stone arena. "That's the Circus of Burnt Skulls. They hold executions there every week. Keeps the public entertained. And keeps them in linc."

"Executing who?"

"Criminals, political prisoners, cannibal tribespeople, or just enslaved laborers if no one else is handy."

Aleck shuddered. "Executed how?" he asked, realizing as the words left his mouth how ghoulish the question was.

Akaz seemed unfazed. "Burning, impalement, trolls, deck-reavers, you name it."

Aleck felt sick. "So there's no clown car."

Ignoring him, Akaz stared into the distance. "Goromath lays claim to the whole island. But he'll never tame it all."

"What island?"

"This island."

"We're on an island?"

"We're on an island," said Akaz.

"Oh." Aleck looked at the horizon all around. "I had no idea Apraxos was such a bigwig. I thought he was just some creep."

"He's the biggest creep we've got. He feeds on the suffering he inflicts."

"What do you mean, feeds on it?"

"I mean literally. With the Rites of Augermath. Vampiric magic. Other people's suffering, physical or emotional, keeps him immortal, fuels his magic."

"But Goromath is the one in charge?"

"In name only. Goromath is 'Supreme Ruler of All Remaining Lands' — which, since the Great Breach, means just the Isle of Kaios. As far as anyone here knows, everything else sank. Any-way, Goromath is smart, sure, but not like Apraxos. He's a good figurehead, but he's a puppet for the most part." Akaz chuckled. "I'd love to spy on their private meetings."

"Wait. You said the Normals were even worse. How could they be worse than public executions and the vampire-magic?"

Akaz scoffed. "At least Goromath is honest. He says, 'Do as I say or my Herax will kill you.'"

"And the Normals?"

Akaz gestured with his snout toward a huge, many-spired building straddling the river. "That's the Senate of the Normals. The Senators run things day-to-day: municipal law, commerce, their twisted Kaios Spirit-Tamer cult. As long as Goromath keeps getting slaves and iron for his war, and Apraxos gets blood sacrifices for his Circus, the Senators do as they please. They're the ones who really maintain the status quo. They make it easy for the Herax; otherwise it'd be nonstop insurrection."

Aleck looked over the city's near-empty evening streets, try-ing to make out the lone figures staggering through the shadows. He wondered what it must be like to live in this bleak and beau-tiful place. The setting sun played its light over the landscape. In the forest, Aleck thought he saw a pattern of parallel ridges. He looked around and could swear he saw, yes, concentric circles surrounding the *God-Dog*.

"Hey Akaz, I think I'm hallucinating."

"Oh?"

"I see circles in the trees." He pointed along a ridge.

"Yeah, that's the Spiral Mounds."

"What? It's real?"

"The road runs around us a few times on its way down to the bay. The Mounds run alongside the road. Or vice-versa, rather; the Mounds were there first."

Aleck looked out toward the water, across the series of curved, wooded ridges. Through occasional clearings in the trees he glimpsed an ancient cobblestone road running between the parallel banks. Turning in a slow circle, he traced the landscape with his gaze. The mounds spiraled outward three times, then reversed direction to curve in toward something under the bay. The shoreline cut that second spiral in half, the Mounds swept away by the tide. Aleck thought he could see faint tracings of the road, intact, in the shallows.

"The road is called the Spiral Ride." Aleck realized Akaz was staring angrily at him, and had been for some time. The fires in his eye sockets burned with intensity, roaring in stereo.

"What?" Aleck gestured apologetically. "What did I do?"

"It was his destiny to break the Ride," the Cook croaked quietly to Akaz.

"What?" said Aleck. "I didn't break shit!"

Akaz stared at Aleck.

"We must let it go, Great Akaz. All things are sooner or later destroyed. Surely you understand this better than anyone."

"Okay!" Flames burst from Akaz's mouth towards the Cook. The Cook jumped into the air and flapped away over the treetops. "Don't lecture me on my own shit, it's embarrassing." Akaz looked back out over the Spiral Ride. "So where were we. Those ridges are the Spiral Mounds. And at the far end of the road is the Shrine of the Nubiles."

"Why would anyone make a road like that?"

"It's magic," said Akaz. "It leads to the Shrine of the Nubiles."

"Oh." Aleck's puzzlement persisted, unscathed. "What's the Shrine of the Nubiles?"

"Home of—" began Akaz, then stopped, staring at the bay, apparently lost in thought.

"Home of...."

"Shh."

"What?"

"Shh! I'm thinking!"

Aleck stared at Akaz for a while, then looked out over the water.

"Dammit!" said Akaz. "Apraxos is going to the Shrine. Obvious! With the Ride broken, it's not protected!"

"What?"

"I'm a shit-for-brains. Going there to get healed."

"What, you mean Corpsewater?"

"Not Corpsewater. The Corpsewater Nymph still has the strength to resist him. No, he's going to the Shrine of the Nubiles. The Nymph of the Shrine has healing magic too, even stronger than the Corpsewater Nymph. And if he can make Her use it.... Her suffering is sweeter to him than anyone's."

"Wait, what does he need to get healed for?"

"The Cook stabbed him."

"What? When?"

"Right before you arrived," said Akaz. "That's why we had to dump the Cook into the Corpsewater pool: Apraxos tagged him back."

"What? What happened?"

Akaz stared out at the bay. "We need to get down there and warn her."

"Okeydokey, yeah, sure. Where's my scuba suit?"

"I need a fucking drink," grumbled Akaz. He looked at Aleck. "No scuba suit. You get the *Drownder's Prayer to the Nymph of the Shrine*."

"The what?"

"A magic spell that lets you breathe water."

"What's a Drownder?"

"That's what the Deep Ones call air-breathers."

"Deep Ones."

"Yeah, the folks that live in the sunken half of the city. They're amphibious."

"Oh," said Aleck, numb now and beyond surprise at hearing such a thing.

"The Prayer to the Nymph only works for a while, so don't get lost. Stay with me."

"How can I get lost?" Aleck made a circular gesture at the landscape around them. "It's just one curving line."

"There's distractions along the way. Come on, I need a damn drink. We can't approach this directly, or we're fucked. So let's hurry up and get a digression over with a.s.a.p."

"That makes absolutely zero sense."

"Chaos magic doesn't frickin' 'make sense.'" Akaz leapt down through the trap door. "C'mon."

Aleck looked down. The shadowy attic hallway seemed to shift in the flickering firelight from Akaz's eyes.

"And close that door," said Akaz, "in case She makes a storm or something."

•

Outside the windows, the land and sky grew dark. Lamplight flickered inside. Akaz, shrunk to the size of a German Shepherd, perched on a heavy wooden stool while Aleck puttered around behind the ancient wooden bar. "My bowl's back there some-where."

Among the mismatched jugs, mugs, and bottles, Aleck found a large ceramic dish that he could only describe as a dog bowl. Glazed black, it bore the name "AKAZ" on the side in red.

"Whiskey," said Akaz.

"What's it look like?"

"You don't know what whiskey looks like?"

Aleck shrugged. "My dad probably let me taste it, but I forget. I don't like alcohol. Makes you stupid."

"Brown," sneered Akaz.

"Brown jug?"

"Brown liquid. Maple syrup color."

Aleck scowled, grabbed a bottle of maple-colored liquid, uncorked it and sniffed. It smelled like gasoline. "I don't know about this stuff." He dumped a large swig into the bowl and placed it in front of Akaz. Akaz put his paws on the bar, put his nose in the bowl, and sniffed.

"Nope." Akaz slurped a mouthful. "Blech," tongue lolling out. "That's that Normal Scotch rotgut. Dump it."

"Where?" Aleck looked around for a sink. He spotted a likely bucket, but hesitated.

"I don't know, on the floor, who cares?"

Aleck shrugged and did so. The thin liquid spread out across the warped floorboards and sank into the cracks between them. "Doesn't 'Scotch' mean it's from Scotland?"

"They don't call it 'Scotch,' I call it 'Scotch.'"

"Yeah but *why'd* you call it that?"

"Why do ya think? 'Cause it tastes like cheap blended Scotch. Less with the questions and more finding me something worth drinking."

Annoyed, Aleck tried a second bottle, shaped differently, its contents slightly darker. Smelled like gasoline. He replaced the bowl in front of Akaz and tipped some liquor into it.

Akaz took a whiff of it. "Ah." He quickly lapped it up. "More."

Aleck poured out another swig.

"More, more, come on, I'm tryna have a drink here."

Aleck upended the bottle to splash into the bowl and waited for Akaz to tell him to stop, which he did not. "What do I do with this?" Aleck held the empty bottle.

"Why not throw it over there." Akaz pointed his nose at the front door before burying it in the bowl of whiskey and slurping it splashily up. Yellow-blue flames licked up the edges of the bowl.

Jerk, thought Aleck. The voices of evening-birds came in through the open doorframe of smoke-darkened woodcarvings. Aleck considered. At worst he would have to sweep up the glass. He flung the bottle over the bar.

As it arced through the air, a tough-looking boy stepped into the doorway. Glass shattered across his boots.

"Hoy!" he said. "What now?"

"Sorry." Aleck did not like the look of this kid. At least his own age, and much sturdier.

Two more boys appeared. Taller and thicker than the people of Corpsewater, these three wore plain gray outfits; glass crunched under their heavy black shoes as they entered. Aleck noticed they carried rucksacks and held unadorned walking sticks.

The first boy spoke. "If that's your idea of hospitality, scar-face, then let's match it." He held up his walking stick in both hands.

Aleck froze, glad to be behind a barricade.

"No fighting in the bar," growled Akaz.

"A talking dog!" said another of the boys.

"He's a Wilder, you fool," said the third.

"Out," said Akaz.

"We want drinks!" The first boy lowered his stick. "We're going to the Shrine!"

"Go on, then. Get out of here."

"We want a drink! The tradition of Kaios Spirit-Tamer

says we can have a drink at the *God-Dog!*"

"Kaios the *Summoner!* He never tamed anything or any-one!"

"The tradition holds, regardless of trivialities of doctrine! We were told by the boys a year older than us, now men, that we get drinks!"

"Wrong. These days you get advice, that's it. First, don't shortcut across the Mounds. Second, watch out for the False Shrines."

"That's only a story," said one of the boys. "There aren't any False Shrines."

"We don't want your Wilder advice," sneered another. "We aren't scared of you dog-apes."

Akaz slurped up a mouthful of whiskey and spat a huge gout of flame into the middle of the room. Aleck felt its heat on his face. The boys ran.

"Damn Normals," said Akaz.

"There are False Shrines?" Aleck came out from behind the bar and closed the door. He took a stool beside Akaz.

"Plenty. That's where the Nubiles are. Sorting through them to the real one, that was the Nymph's whole idea when she set it up. Teaching the truth of love and sex or some shit."

"Sex?" Aleck felt intrigued and nervous.

"But the Normals like the False Shrines so much, they never even get to the Nymph."

"Oh. But what makes them False Shrines?"

"Ask her." Akaz returned to his whiskey. "It's her thing. I can't explain it."

•

They walked hurriedly down the dark cobblestone road, under a black sky crowded with stars enough to light their way. The Cook crossed back and forth above them on his wide black wings. Their path curved endlessly to the right, between ridges of stone and soil too high to see over, overgrown with trees, past occasional cairns of stacked boulders. Sometimes they saw shrines of salvaged rubble, housing broken statues. Offerings of flowers, food, and small trinkets adorned these structures, but Akaz never let Aleck inspect them beyond grabbing a piece of fruit now and then as they passed.

"Are these the Shrines of the Nubiles?"

"No." Akaz laughed at him. "Those are all underwater, at the far end of the road, like I said. Come on."

"If we're in a hurry, why don't we just go straight there? This is taking us like fifty times as long."

"We can't cut across, *even though* the goddamn road's magic is goddamn broken." Akaz glared at him, then looked away. "Because I can't attack Apraxos directly without being cursed with bad luck. I can't even approach him in a straight line."

"Why?"

"It's goddamn weird magic, that's why! Stop whining and walk!"

Aleck fumed quietly, but not for long. The surroundings demanded his attention. Mount Kaios, looming on the horizon, circled around as they progressed: behind them, then in front, then passing for a long time on their left with the thousand-foot-high face of Kaios staring down. The evening air grew cooler.

"He's kind of menacing."

Akaz glanced up at the great stone face. "He was pissed off that day. Some of the Wilders want to destroy that face." Akaz gestured with his snout toward the sky. "Our man Cook sure does."

"Really? I thought they liked Kaios."

"Yeah exactly. They think it's depressing. They think he carved it in a moment of weakness."

"So why don't they, I dunno, avalanche it? How do you knock a giant stone face off a mountain around here?"

"They could do it, but the Herax guard it pretty seriously. Apraxos claims it's a 'cultural treasure.' In reality, though, he just likes how demoralizing it is. Big Brother psych terror aesthetics shit."

From around the bend in the road appeared a weathered wooden structure. It looked to Aleck like a large boat, prow upward, half buried in the side of the mound. "What's that?"

"A Wilder shrine to keep Herax away."

"How do you mean?"

"You'll see."

Soon Aleck saw indeed, a weatherbeaten old ship, not unlike a Viking longboat, prow pointing upward at the sky, stern buried deep in the side of the mound. Its mast loomed most of the way across the road. Spears jutted from the hull like the spines of a hedgehog, pinning dozens of skeletons in place. Pelts were tacked up all over the deck. The Cook landed on the end of the mast and faced the deck, bobbing, eyes shut. Aleck watched the crow pray.

"Those are Herax skeletons," said Akaz.

"And all the furs?" Aleck gestured at the pelts.

"Hides of Wilder warriors who died fighting the Herax."

"Wilders? Like the Cook?"

Akaz nodded. "A pack of Wilder geomancers made the Spiral Mounds."

"But Cook's got feathers, not fur."

"Bah. In wolf form he has fur."

Aleck looked over the wrecked boat. The pelts and skeletons adorned it like the garlands on the other shrines they'd passed.

"So how does this keep Herax away?"

"It's a reminder of the truce, and the cost of breaking it. And a reminder of the magic of the Ride. The Spiral Ride was built as a sacred path to the Shrine; you're supposed to walk it from one end to the other without stopping. Crossing the mounds is taboo. Taboo and bad luck. Even if you're flying."

Aleck looked up at the Cook, now circling overhead, flying back and forth across the road. "What the hell are you talking about?"

Akaz laughed. "I don't mean birds. Birds are free. I mean a flying Herax ship."

"This?" Aleck gestured with both hands at the longboat skeleton-shrine. "This flies?"

"Not anymore," said Akaz. "Anyway, you can only cross the spiral under special circumstances."

"Like what?"

"Like if it's your goddamn destiny to do so, I guess," grumbled Akaz.

Whatever that means. Aleck shook his head. "Aren't we in a hurry to warn the Nymph? I thought you said the spiral was already broken. Why don't we just cut across?"

"What, and break it even worse? I'm trying to salvage it here!"

"Okay, okay!" Aleck felt put off by Akaz's intensity. "So what if you don't break the taboo? What if they just follow the road here?" He gestured down the curve of cobblestones.

"Herax can't do that either. Not in their ships. The Nymph decreed that any being could freely travel the length of the Ride; that's integral to the nature of the Shrine. That freedom extends to the spirits trapped in the masts and sails of the Herax ships. They're how Herax ships fly, enslaved air elementals. Spirits go free, ships fall."

"Whoa."

"It happened a bunch of times, back in the day. Apraxos kept trying different enchantments, none of them strong enough. Not with the Ride intact." Akaz stared at the wrecked boat, lost in thought. He put his snout to the cobblestones and sniffed, looked down the Ride, sniffed again. He shook his head and muttered. "Fucking damaged, all right."

"What happened when the ships fell?" Aleck felt eager to stay away from that subject. *'It was his destiny to break the Ride,'* the Cook had said. *What the hell did that mean?*

Akaz sighed. Little licks of flame darted out of his nostrils. "Hypothetically, any Herax who survived the fall would have been free to walk the length of the Spiral. But anyway, back then Wilders didn't typically bother waiting for a boat to fall. They'd just attack on sight."

"How do Wilders attack a flying boat?"

Akaz gestured with his nose at the shrine covered in skeletons. "Herax are organized, but Wilders are unpredictable. And *fast*."

"There's a lot of Wilder pelts up there, though." Aleck watched the Cook alight again on the mast and resume praying.

"Those are pelts from *all* the Wilders who have died fighting Herax. Ever. Whereas those bones are just a handful of token Herax dead. All that's left of the hundreds they killed before Goromath granted sovereignty of Bitchwood to the Wilders."

"So where are the rest of the Herax skeletons?"

"Ever give a dog a bone?" Akaz laughed.

"Huh?"

"They don't just gnaw on 'em, they chew them up till there's nothing left."

Aleck's gaze darted from the wreck to the Cook to Akaz. "They—they *ate* their *bones?*" He shuddered, looking over the unmistakably humanoid Herax skeletons. He looked again at Akaz, and at the Cook.

"Why do you think he's called the Cannibal-King?" Akaz laughed some more.

Aleck felt queasy, as though he'd just passed through another teleportation doorway.

"You gotta understand the difference between the cannibal tribes. The Wilders of the woods, the Givers of the desert, the Deepest of the water, they only eat unwelcome visitors to their lands. The Herax of the air, though, they eat for sport. They breed people for food." Akaz paused. "Well, Givers breed people too, but the Cannibal-King is supposedly gonna cure them of that."

"Why would I want to help summon *any* Cannibal-King? He sounds like the last sorta guy I'd want to help conquer a country."

"Look, maybe you think you can get the Witch-Queen to leave the safety of Gomothrax and fly across the bay to join us?"

"Who what?"

Flames licked out of Akaz's mouth. "Sorry, not gonna happen! So we're gonna need our Cannibal-King. And I'm telling ya, he is the exact sorta guy who'll *stop* the Givers from breeding bipedal livestock. The sorta guy that can unite the wild folk against the Herax, and free the damn Isle of Kaios. You think the Digglies and Deep Ones are going to do it?"

Aleck narrowed his eyes. "You saying they don't have the will to seek their own, like, liberation?"

"Not talking about will. Picture the folks from Corpsewater fighting a flying boat. It flies over the palisade. Two dozen villagers shake their sticks in the air. Two dozen javelins rain down on them. Then another two dozen, and another, and another."

Aleck frowned. "Don't they have, like, bow-and-arrows?"

Akaz shook his head. "Slings. They have slings, for hunting birds and squirrels. Fuck you up if you're unarmored, sure, but they're not war weapons." He nodded toward the Cook, who still stood on the tip of the mast, bobbing. "Wilders have bows, though, and they can put an arrow in your eye, helmet or no helmet. While hopping on one foot. Those guys can fight the Herax. Especially in coordination with the Givers." His ears shot straight up. "What's that?"

Aleck listened, but heard nothing. "What?" He jumped as a black blur dove past his head: the Cook disappearing into the trees.

"Look out!" Akaz sprinted behind the shrine. Aleck looked around and saw nothing, although in the distance he heard something. Someone screaming? He ran for the shrine, keeping one eye on the road. As he ducked behind a bush he saw the three Normal boys from the *God-Dog* come around the bend, sprinting full-tilt back down the road.

Behind and above them, between them and the starry night, flew a one-masted boat, shaped exactly like the anti-Herax shrine. This one, however, gleamed with black lacquer, two dozen living Herax spearmen aboard, covered in black leather armor. The longboat glowed with torches and lanterns. Aleck saw a metal cage on the deck, filled with women howling in lamentation. Their skin looked blue in the firelight. Aleck cowered behind the bush. A Herax soldier in the bow flung a harpoon, spearing one of the boys through the back. Soldiers hauled the screaming boy onto the deck and dove onto him. From behind the bulwark came the unmistakable sounds of them eating him alive. Aleck gagged, forcing down his vomit lest he give himself away.

Broad-winged crows erupted from the dark trees on either side of the road, flapping and cawing, soaring at the boat. As they neared the torchlit deck, they transformed into huge wolves in midair, snatching Herax soldiers by the wrist or throat in their snarling jaws and wrestling them overboard. Falling wolves turned back into crows while the Herax dropped to the road. On the ground, more wolves piled onto broken-limbed Herax, tearing them apart. Blood slicked their fur.

The Herax boat veered off the road. As it passed overhead, Aleck saw water dripping heavily from the hull. The crows flew at the boat again, but all turned aside at the last moment. They attacked again, and again turned sharply away, deflected by some unseen force. As the longboat flew away toward the Zone of the Herax, Aleck saw a robed figure in the stern lit by flickering torchlight, gloved hands outstretched in a warding gesture, each holding something like an irregular golden bowl.

"There's Apraxos," said Akaz. "And those were Nubiles in that cage. Some of them, anyway."

"Was the Nymph there?"

"Not sure."

"How come the spirits didn't come out of the sails?"

"I reckon it's because the Ride," Akaz said with an air of quiet menace, "is broken."

The Cook flew down to them and changed to man-form: bark-gray skin, leaf-green hair, naked. Seething. "Apraxos. With the Skull. Even with it broken in two, he could use it to tame us aside."

"Skull?" asked Aleck. "What skull?"

"The Skull of Kaios," said Akaz. "He can use it to control spirits. That's how he trapped your spirit in the astral plane, when you were on your way in."

"He's got, like, Kaios's actual *Skull?*"

"Yeah. There's them kids." Akaz pointed his nose at the two boys from the *God-Dog*. "The remaining ones, anyway."

The Cook leapt into the air and flapped away on black wings.

Aleck saw both boys wandering in the road, crying. One was the boy who had threatened him. Both had lost their walking sticks, and one had dropped his backpack as well. "What should we do?"

"Hey!" said Akaz. "Go home!"

The boys started running for cover, then recognized Akaz. "You have to help us get Stathan back!"

"Wake up, asshole. Your friend is dead. Eaten. Not only his body, but his soul along with it. So you won't see him in his next life, either, 'cause he won't have one."

The boys wailed.

"And since it looks like those Herax took the Nubiles, there's no sense in continuing your original plan, 'cause there's no sex to be had at the end of the road. Not that you're in any sort of shape for it anyway. So go home, don't come back."

"Please!"

"Shut up and listen. You came down the Spiral Ride to grow up a little. Didn't happen the way you hoped? Tough luck, take it as a gift. You're still alive, and now you know something about real life: it's going to end, and you never know when, and best not to have it happen because you're doing something fuckin' stupid. Even Kaios the Summoner died. Arguably, doing something stupid." Akaz ended with, "Go home," his voice a thunderclap.

The boys fled.

•

Aleck and Akaz stood at the water's edge. The Spiral Mounds sloped into the bay. Dark waters spread before them, with darker hills silhouetted beyond. At the horizon's low point, Aleck again saw the spire he had spotted from the rooftop: not quite so tiny now, it looked like a castle with tall towers, minuscule lights twinkling in its distant windows. Wait, what did Akaz say was across the bay? A Witch-Queen? And some other nonsense word. The name of her castle?

Aleck saw pale light sparkling on the waves of the bay. He turned to see that the sun had risen above Mount Kaios, into the lower fringes of an overcast morning sky.

Aleck forgot all about the castle across the bay. "Wait! We didn't walk all night, no way! That felt more like an hour!"

"Time moves funny in the Spiral Mounds. Plus the Ride's broken, so who knows how that affects it. Let's hope we only lost the one night."

"Isn't there a quicker way we could have come?"

Akaz gave him no heed and stared at the water.

"Why would she have healed him? It doesn't make sense. I don't get it."

"Who said it was voluntary," Akaz said quietly.

"Oh." Aleck wondered how that worked. He looked at Akaz. Akaz stared out over the water. Eager to rid the situation of its gravity, Aleck said, "Breathing water was cool, back in Corpse-water, but I didn't exactly get a chance to enjoy it. What do I do?"

Akaz stared at him for a moment, then looked away and shook his head, ears flapping. Stared back at Aleck for a bit.

Then, "Repeat after me. This is a stanza from the *Book of the Cannibal-King:*

> *For the Drownder can pray to the Nymph of the Shrine*
> *And she gives him the strength to breathe water*
> *And she, the Dragons' first daughter*
> *Will upon him her Victories shine:*
> *The gift of the Nymph to the Drownders above,*
> *The spiritual act of physical love."*

As Aleck stumbled through the last line, a woman emerged from the bay, clutching a nondescript gray robe around her. The first direct sunlight of the day broke through the clouds to fall upon her. Pulling back her soaked hood, she stared at Akaz, shaking. Her skin and hair shone blue-green; her forehead had a prominent lateral scar, right in the middle, two inches across. Its edges looked jagged, as though the wound had been crudely sewn shut long ago. Despite her strange appearance, Aleck was most struck by her deep frown and the intense worry in her eyes. He had never seen anyone who looked so devastatingly sad. She still dripped baywater, but Aleck felt sure that tears also poured down her face. Her gaze remained on Akaz for a long while.

"Did you see my Nubiles?" she asked, eventually.

"Yes," said Akaz. "I'm relieved you weren't among them."

"I am touched by your compassion." She spoke with cold sarcasm.

"I can help you find them."

The blue-green woman stood there for a long while, looking around at nothing in particular, arms crossed tightly.

"Apraxos the Watcher came to me injured," said the woman. "Stabbed. He was... *insistent*... that I heal him."

"I am sorry."

"Do you know how he came to be wounded?" She gave Akaz an intense stare.

Akaz looked away. "Wasn't me."

The woman looked past Aleck's shoulder. "You!" She snarled, pointing savagely. Aleck turned and saw the Cook flapping away.

Aleck turned back to her. "I can help you find your Nubiles, too."

The woman looked at Aleck, and to his surprise, she smiled. "You are here so soon, Young Aleck."

"Yeah, well," said Akaz, "that's Weird Luck for you."

"Wha—?" asked Aleck. "How do you know my name?"

"Never mind that," said Akaz.

"You have not explained to him...?" The Nymph seemed astonished.

"You let me do my thing my way, and I'll help you get your Nubiles back."

"How? Will you send your apprentice up against Apraxos?" She nodded at Aleck.

"What!?" asked Aleck. "Is that how the Cook got hurt? You sent him to fight what's-his-name for you?"

"NO! I don't want to talk about it."

"You knew, then," said the Nymph. "You knew he was hurt, and that he might therefore seek me."

"Yeah. This is us coming to warn you." Akaz lowered his head, squinting up at her. "Sorry we're late."

The Nymph clutched herself more tightly, clenched and unclenched her jaw. "I'm sure I will forgive you. In time. As always."

"Can we go save the Nubiles?"

"Yes," said the Nymph. "And come along swiftly, if you speak the truth about aiding me. Aside from the strength the Watcher has just taken from me, I weaken away from my Shrine or my River for long, even if only to walk the length of beach between them." She struggled up the side of the Mound, stood silhouetted against the dawn with the trees.

Akaz turned to Aleck. "Come on." He followed the Nymph.

Aleck climbed the slope of rocky dirt. "Wait. Aren't we crossing the spiral thingy?"

Akaz gestured with his head at the Nymph. "It's her spell, dude. We're kinda exempt when she's *with* us."

"Oh." Aleck shook his head. "Obviously. Of course." He followed them down the slope.

•

A beach of rocks ran alongside the bay. Boulders lined the edge between beach and forest, rising ahead into low, craggy cliffs with stone houses atop them. They walked up the thin strand of beach, Aleck trudging behind Akaz and the Nymph as they argued. The Cook circled distantly overhead.

"How did they get the Nubiles?" asked Akaz.

"They flew in and took them."

"They flew down out of the sky and under the water?"

"Yes."

"But Herax hate water! How did they breathe? You've kept your spell from Apraxos, right?"

Aleck saw her nod. "I have kept it from him. But he summoned such a wind around the ship that a bubble of air enclosed it."

"Fuck. That's a first." Akaz looked up at the Nymph. "You ever seen that before?"

"No."

They walked in silence for a while. Aleck envisioned the attack, and found the thought of Apraxos increasingly frightening.

"When he had finished healing himself," she said hollowly, "and stole my Nubiles, the Watcher announced to us that he scoffed at our Cannibal-King. He said that he was taking the Nubiles to punish us." She stopped and looked at Akaz. "'To punish you damned rebels,' he said."

Akaz scowled.

"You understand what this means?" The Nymph spoke through clenched teeth.

"It means he's a vengeful prick."

"It means that Apraxos sought to punish me for *your* deeds, Akaz." Her eyes welled with new tears. "I have nothing to do with your waterless Giver army, or its grim prophecies; nor the insurgent Wilders, embodiers of your soot and fur and fire, except when they fish in my river."

"Look, I'm sorry he took the kids, but you're in this. I'm doing it for you, goddammit!"

"How could even you, in your madness, imagine such a

thing, when I have begged you again and again to stop?"

"'The kids'?" asked Aleck.

"Let's just get them back, and we can debate wartime ethics after."

Did Aleck understand correctly that Akaz and the Nymph were somehow the parents of the Nubiles?

"Nonsense." She sobbed, voice cracking. "The path chosen determines the destination. Meanwhile, I am certain he intends to perform the Rites of Augermath upon them, and use their souls to power an evil spell. Only in opposition to your needless, bloodthirsty plot!" She grimaced, and tears spilled down her cheeks.

"To your last point," said Akaz, "you know as well as anyone that Apraxos uses the Rites without provocation."

The Nymph closed her eyes.

"How many did he get?" asked Akaz.

"Five."

"So only a few. That's not so bad."

"They are each unique!" The Nymph glared at Akaz. "Just as every creature or spirit! Unique and irreplaceable!"

"Okay! I just mean in terms of how much damage he can do with them!"

"Infinite damage," she said. "Five times infinity."

They walked down the beach in silence for a bit.

"Did Apraxos hurt you?" Aleck asked the Nymph.

She smiled at him again. "Only my feelings, dear boy."

Aleck didn't think she looked well at all, however. "Are you sure?"

Her smile waned. Aleck looked at Akaz, who said nothing.

In the distance, the beach met the mouth of the river. Beside the river, under the cliffs, sat what looked like a hundred colored tents.

"What's that?"

"My blessed river," said the Nymph. "Those are the booths of the V'Ghulia Markets: the Bayside Market of the Deep Ones, and the Riverside Market of the Shallow Ones."

"What's the difference between Deeps and Shallows?"

"There are cultural differences."

"Class differences," said Akaz.

"The songs of the Deep Ones celebrate fellowship and simple pleasures. Whereas the Shallow Ones' culture seeks to imitate the Normals in their pursuit and display of personal wealth, and even to outdo them."

"What the heck does that mean?"

"It means the Shallow Ones are assholes," said Akaz.

"You cannot condemn an entire people." The Nymph limped ahead. "Their lives are out of harmony, but they suffer for it."

"I'll condemn the whole Herax, thank you very much, and as many other entire peoples as I damn well please. Shallows and Normals are assholes for occupying their social position, even if there are a few who wish for a better world."

"Their songs have led them away from the heart of life." The Nymph seemed wistful. "The Shallows and Normals prefer elaborate pleasures, and have forgotten the source of true joy."

"What's the source of true joy?" asked Aleck.

The Nymph turned, looked him in the eye, and smiled warmly. "You will know it in your heart if you earnestly seek it." Then her frown returned. Turning around, she hastened onward, her limp easing as she approached the river. They followed her down the strand. The cliff overlooking them almost resembled the face of a lamenting demon.

•

The canopies of the V'Ghulia Market drew slowly closer, and Aleck discerned distant figures moving among them. The beach turned sandy as they approached the river. He kicked off his sneakers, enjoying the cold sand on his bare feet. The Nymph now walked tall and strong, without any limp at all.

"Hey I have a question," he asked the Nymph. "So my name is in the prophecies about the First Herald and whatever? Like it really says 'Aleck'?"

"No, nothing of the sort." The Nymph laughed.

"How do you know my name, then?"

"Ut—" said Akaz.

"Your future self is here," said the Nymph.

"Hey!" said Akaz. "Zip it!"

"He came back in time with his wife," she said. "Your wife. I recognized you by the scars of your face. He is decades older than you, but the scars are unmistakable."

"Wow. Far out." Aleck looked at Akaz. "Why didn't you want her to tell me that?"

"Because if you meet them, there can be all kinds of trouble. Paradoxes. Something could happen to you and change their past. Worst case scenario, the Reality Patrol notices, and you definitely don't want them to show up."

"Reality Patrol."

"They bust people," said Akaz, "who do things like try to meet their future selves."

"There's a 'Reality Patrol'?"

"Actually, the real *worst* case scenario is you trigger a pan-dimensional Train Wreck."

"Train wreck."

"That's what happens when you stretch the membrane between the worlds to the breaking point. Crossing or looping too many lines of Fate — like, for example, meeting a goddamn version of yourself from another time or parallel dimension."

"What's the 'train wreck' part?"

"A big frickin' mess is what. Gates popping open like holes in Swiss cheese, all sorts of motherfucking things jumping in and out of them. I've been in a Train Wreck, and I don't aim to repeat it."

"Whoa," said Aleck. "Okay, okay."

"Come along!" The Nymph turned and continued down the strand toward the markets. Aleck and Akaz followed.

"The way it is now, we know you grow up into Old Aleck and come back here. If something changes the course of your life, say, something like *meeting yourself*, you might not come back. We can't have that. We need him."

"What for? What's he doing here?"

"That's what I'm telling you! I can't say or it'll skew things! Deviate from your destiny, next thing we know you slip on a banana peel and break your neck, and he disappears like was never here, because he wasn't. And I need him!"

"That could happen whether I run into him or not, though. I

could die a year from now, back in New Jersey, in my bathtub."

"But you *don't*. We know that. Your future self is *here*."

"So what do we do?"

"Well my first goddamn choice was, 'Don't tell the kid.'" Akaz glowered at the Nymph, then looked back at Aleck. "Because who knows how that knowledge is going to affect you now. I bet this very moment you're thinking you can meet them anyway, and it won't turn into a disaster."

"No I'm not! Where are they?" Aleck himself felt that he had asked, perhaps, too hastily.

"See? Exactly! He's off somewhere quiet, finishing his book, and wherever he is, you're not going."

"He's writing a book? I mean, I'm gonna write a book?"

"Yeah, a guidebook to the city. That's what he came back in time for."

"Why?"

"Look, how about you focus on making sure you don't run into him."

They caught up to the Nymph.

"He should have a Keeper robe," she said.

"What's that?"

"The Keepers of the Archive," she indicated her nondescript gray clothes, "enspell their garments with a charm of innocuousness."

"The who whats their what with a what?"

The Nymph pulled her hood up and walked to the edge of the water. Aleck stared at her.

"Wait." He turned to Akaz. "What was I just saying—?"

Akaz laughed. "Beats me."

"What's so funny?" Aleck looked up and down the beach. "Hey, wasn't your friend here?"

"Who?"

"I forget...."

"Then how the hell am I supposed to know who you're talking about?" Akaz laughed louder.

"Your underwater friend! She was just here! Wait, who's that?" Aleck pointed at the hooded Nymph.

"That's just one of them Keepers. They're harmless, everyone knows that."

"Who are they?"

"Monks. Scholars."

"Oh." Aleck stared at the Nymph. She turned around, pulled back her hood, and started walking back to them. "Hey! There you are! Wait, what the hell just happened?"

They continued up the beach. "The robe is magic, as I described. It makes its wearer innocuous."

"Holy smokes. You could shoplift a whole watermelon with that thing."

"Speaking of which," said Akaz, "here's the market."

Up ahead, Aleck saw a walkway of weatherbeaten old boards. A handful of green-bearded men with blue-green skin sat there talking.

"Watch out for spies." Akaz shrank to the size of a German Shepherd. "And watch out for Old Aleck. You see him, you just walk the other way. I'm serious."

"How do I even know what he looks like? What I look like. What I will look like."

Akaz spat a little wisp of flame. "Like the Nymph said, you've gotta pretty damn recognizable face now, Aleck."

"Oh." Aleck touched his scars.

The Nymph put up her hood. Now that he knew, Aleck could keep track of her, with effort; but the magic of the robe continuously tried to omit her from his awareness.

As they got closer, Aleck realized the men's green beards were actually elaborate fronds dangling from their gill-like noses. The Deep Ones had long, webbed fingers and toes, and wore nothing but shell jewelry and fish-skin harnesses hung with bone tools. Aleck felt uncomfortably scrutinized by their huge eyes.

"That's a good-looking dog," said one of them, in a languid accent.

"Uh, thanks." Aleck tried to hurry past without seeming rude.

"Nice scars," said the Deep One. "You get them in a fight?"

"No, car crash. Uh, I gotta go, man, later."

"You should walk slow," called the Deep One after them. "Hurrying in the morning is bad luck, little Drownder."

They walked past knots of Deep Ones chatting around displays of miscellaneous objects. Aleck saw tools, jewelry, and ornaments carved from bone and shell, arranged upon blankets or bare ground. Soon they approached the first of the booths. A wide, open-sided tent of blue silk billowed in the wind from the bay; beneath it, low wicker tables lay heaped with bizarre fish and seafood. Aleck saw fully-dressed Deep Ones paying in metal coin and staggering away under the weight of large baskets. More booths clustered beyond.

"Who are the guys with pants on?"

"Servants of the Normals," said Akaz.

"Are any of these Shallow Ones?"

"These are all Deep Ones."

"Shallows lack the gill-fronds," said the Nymph.

"They're a different species?"

"No," said Akaz. "They hack them off."

Aleck winced. "Can they still breathe water?"

"A bit."

"Just 'a bit'? Why the hell do they do it, then? Does it hurt?"

"They prefer to more closely resemble the Drownder tribe of the Normals," said the Nymph. "They believe doing so will make them happy."

"Sounds fucked up and then some."

"No shit," said Akaz. "Look, enough amphibian anthropology. We've got Nubiles to find." The crowd around them thickened. They heard criers ringing bells in the distance. "How did they take them?"

"With nets," said the Nymph.

"What? Why didn't the Nubiles just turn to water and flow through the mesh?"

"Apraxos carried the Skull of Kaios. He tamed them into solid form. Did you know the Skull has been broken in halves?"

"Yeah." Akaz sounded glum. "I hope we can still use it. If we can even retrieve it."

"Use it for what?" asked Aleck.

"I hope you neither obtain nor use it," said the Nymph.

Akaz ignored her. "Old Aleck and I need it for our project," he said to Aleck.

"Why don't we just go get it now, while we're saving the Nubiles?"

"If we can, but easier said than done. They're probably in the Herax Zone by now."

"So? What about the robes?"

"The robes make the wearer innocuous, not invisible," said the Nymph.

"We could get into the Herax Zone by way of the tunnels under the city, but even with robes, I don't know how you'd get out. Keepers don't just wander freely around the Herax Zone, climbing in and outta tunnels."

An approaching bell-ringer proclaimed: "Nymphs of the Shrine at the Circus today! Nymphs of the Shrine on display!"

"Well, there ya go," said Aleck. "Weirdlucky, no?"

"Yeah, yeah."

The Nymph stood weeping with her face in her hands.

"He means that stadium you showed me this morning?"

"The Circus of Burnt Skulls," said Akaz. "A lot easier to get into than the Zone of the Herax, but again, I don't know how we'd get back out. It'll be full of Herax, and we'll be dragging a herd of giggling Nubiles."

"Nymphs of the Shrine," cried the bell-ringer, "Nymphs on display! Come to the Circus today!"

"Where is it?"

"Up the river." Akaz gestured with his snout.

•

As far as Aleck could tell, the Shallow Ones looked just like the Deep Ones, aside from their attire and the missing gill-fronds. From living in the U.S.A. he was accustomed to thinking of caste based on skin color, but their skin varied along the same spectrum of blues and greens. Many of the Shallow Ones wore lavish garments resembling tangles of loose silk ribbon, which Aleck could envision flowing beautifully underwater; others wore ornamented robes and jackets. The Shallow One merchants of Riverside Market had much more elaborate booths than the Deep Ones of the bay side, including many permanent structures of carved wood. Aleck thought he saw the very same ornaments and seafood for sale, however. *Paying twice as much for the same shit, I'm sure,* thought Aleck, *just 'cause it's on a shelf instead of a blanket, and the clerk has a more uptight outfit.*

A stone bridge crossed the mouth of the river, with a freestanding archway marking the entrance to it. The Nymph stopped and stared at the sculpted arch. Aleck saw bas-reliefs of creatures resembling squid and octopi, interwoven with images of women with tentacles for arms and legs.

"I can go no further. Whether you are able to free them or not, meet me in Billycutter's Tunnel, as soon as you can."

"Huh? I thought we were sneaking into the Circus!"

"I cannot go with you. I cannot long survive so far inland."

"What? Wait, no, that sucks."

The Nymph took a talisman from a pocket in her robe and handed it to Aleck: a seashell with a tiny hole drilled through it and faint, indecipherable carvings upon its inner surface. "Kaios called this his Token of Time Dilation. He fashioned it when he was young. If you hold it in your mouth, you will move a hundred times more swiftly than the world around you."

"I was wondering what happened to that," said Akaz.

"Whoa," said Aleck, ignoring Akaz. "Are you serious? With this and a robe, I could steal anything from anywhere." Aleck motioned to put it in his mouth.

"Stop! You must only use it once; only once *ever*, and for no longer than a few moments."

"How come?" Aleck felt crestfallen.

"The Token is dangerous. Your mortal body cannot long withstand its power. Overuse will age and wither you." She plucked a blue-green hair from her head and threaded the Token onto it.

"Have you used it?"

"Yes. Twice. And even though I am immortal, the second time so weakened me that Apraxos was able to then trap me in the river and bay." She tied the Token around Aleck's neck and kissed him on the mouth, then slipped off her robe and handed it to him. The Nymph pointed her finger in Akaz's face. "No killing."

Akaz shook his head no. "I'm going to do what I have to."

The Nymph scowled at him, then looked at Aleck. "Please. No killing, not even a Herax." She turned and dove into the river.

In a little while Aleck realized that he had been staring after her. He glanced to see if Akaz had noticed. Akaz stared at the river.

Blood Eagle

Watcher, beware
The First Herald:
Running faster than wind,
He steals your nymphs.
He frees the Second Herald
From you even as you watch.

Watcher, beware
The Second Herald,
Destined to serve the King.
Fast as fire,
He feeds upon your children
In your own home.

— from "The Song of the Heralds"
by Kaios the Summoner

Aleck and Akaz walked along the river, through the market of the Shallow Ones. The carved wooden booths grew more ornate as they progressed, though the food and objects for sale still looked much the same to Aleck. With the Nymph gone, the Cook stayed near, hopping and flapping from one booth's roof to another. In the distance, Aleck saw the Senate with its tall spires.

"There's one thing I don't get."

"Make it quick," muttored Akaz.

"Isn't it risky for me to do this? What you said about endangering my future self...."

"Old Aleck told me this is how it happened when he was your age. When he was you. So long as we stick to the script, we know it works out. Also, a little audacity should bring out your luck. 'Fortune favors the bold,' as Kaios used to say."

"But what if I slip on a banana peel and break my neck, like you said? At the Circus?"

"Well duh, you still gotta watch where the hell you step," said Akaz.

"What?"

"Don't take Lady Luck for granted, not for a second, I'm telling you."

"But that doesn't make any sense! You're telling me to be reckless and careful at the same time!"

"No," said Akaz. "*Think.* It's two different things. Even if you have a destiny, your fate is still of your own making. Now shut up."

Aleck walked along in silence through the crowd, confused and fuming, continuing the argument in his head. *Goddamn asshole shit-for-brains gibberish-talkin' dog.* Akaz stayed close, his nose occasionally to the ground or sniffing the air. The market crowd thickened, but no one took particular notice of them. Again and again Aleck observed Shallow Ones harassing Deep Ones, then turning to pander to their Normal customers, illustrating the power dynamic Akaz and the Nymph had described.

As they neared the Senate, Aleck realized it stood far larger than he initially thought, straddling the entire river on immense stone pilings. Wide streets ran into it through huge, gaping archways. Although its massiveness impressed him, its design seemed unremarkable, even bland: stark gray walls rose smoothly into tapering towers. After a moment he realized there were no windows anywhere.

"The Senate building is huge," said Aleck.

"That's where the Normal and Shallow One merchants divide their spoils."

"It looks like a prison. What about the Herax? Do they meet there, too?"

"Goromath has a seat in the great hall, but as far as I know, he rarely goes there. When he does he usually sleeps."

"But how does he make sure they're doing what he wants them to?"

"The Senate is happy with the status quo. It's what makes them rich. Now and then someone with different priorities tries to oppose Goromath, but not for long."

"How do you mean?"

"Now and then he just goes ahead and kills 'em on the Senate floor." Akaz chuckled. "That's always exciting. He did it quite a few times when he took over, till he got the point across. That kept them in line for a few hundred years, but lately there's been some dissent, and he's doing it again."

"Whoa."

"Yeah, a few douchebags think they can use my rep for some cheap P.R., attach my brand to some toothless reformist bullshit as their medium of self-aggrandizement. Fuck 'em. Fucker's saving me the trouble of killing them myself."

"Didn't understand a word of that."

"Point is that I hate every last motherfucker in the building. I shed no tears when Goromath shakes one by the neck like a dog with a rag-doll."

"Still," said Aleck. "Harsh."

"Nah. Come on." Akaz led him across a cobblestone street. Clusters of plain, square booths sprawled at the foot of the Senate: the New Market of the Normal merchants. A clamor assaulted Aleck's ears. Bell-ringers shouted over one another to attract customers, some of them wearing signs, swinging bells in both hands, or dancing with bells tied to wrists and ankles. A small crowd surrounded two men, arguing, both in long coats hung with a hundred little bells.

Aleck saw short, wiry Digglies, heavily laden, jostling one another to stay clear of browsing Normal shoppers. Merchants displayed racks of clothing, cases of jewelry, jars of spices. Walking past a table laden with fruit, Aleck shoplifted a black apple. Bell-ringers everywhere announced the Nubiles on display at the Circus.

"Come on," barked Akaz over the din.

Aleck followed him through the crowds and into a huge gate in the Senate building. He looked around for the Cook but couldn't spot any crows. An enormous hall took up the entire bottom floor, sunlight streaming in through many tall, wide archways. Despite its size Aleck found this space louder and even more crowded. Several booths the size of small buildings had large church-bells continuously ringing atop them.

"This is hell!" shouted Aleck.

"What?" asked Akaz.

"Never mind."

"What?" asked Akaz.

Dammit. Fuck crowds. Fuck those goddamn bells. What is wrong with these people.

Aleck followed Akaz around the less-crowded perimeter. They passed outside through one of the arches, exiting onto a wide, crowded street. A row of stone columns ran down the middle, supporting nothing. At the far end of the street, many blocks away, squatted the Circus of Burnt Skulls. Over it circled several Herax longboats; beyond, Aleck saw part of the wall marking the Zone of the Herax. Crowds poured down the street toward the Circus, urged on by more criers: announcing the Tournament for the Nubiles, or proclaiming the addition of something called Blood Eagle to the day's festivities.

As they walked along the row of empty columns, Aleck noticed something strange over the Circus, distinct from the Herax boats: a small shimmer in the air, as from heat or smoke.

"What's that thing hovering over the Circus?" Aleck pointed with his chin.

Akaz looked up. "Boats."

"No, that shimmering."

"Like a big candle flame?"

"Yeah."

"Barely visible in the sunlight?"

"Yeah."

"That's one of the Salamandrines. It's not over the Circus, it's behind the Circus. Floating above one of the guard-towers in the Herax wall. Look down the wall and you'll see more of them."

Aleck stood up. He thought he saw the Cook perched on the corner of a nearby building, but then he saw another oversized crow, and another. *Our guy could be any of them.* He frowned and looked into the distance. Running his gaze down the Herax wall, he saw something shimmering over every tower. He knelt again. "What are Salamandrines?"

"Fire spirits. Minor gods of the Givers. Apraxos captured them all a long time ago and trapped them in spheres of un-melting ice. Now they float over the towers in the Herax wall."

"Unmelting ice?"

"Yes."

"Why doesn't it melt?"

"It's magic, goofus. It doesn't melt."

"What if it did?"

"Then those Salamandrines would go free and burn down the towers. And burn any Herax they could get their hands on."

"So how do we do that?"

"You wish." Akaz flashed a fiery dog-smile. "C'mon."

"Hell yeah I do."

They walked on. Aleck saw more crows, one of them sharpening its beak against a stone gargoyle. Halfway to the Circus, crude busts and statues appeared, crowning the columns that ran down the middle of the street. Every sculpture depicted a glowering warrior, some Herax, some Normal. As they proceeded, the sculptures increased in quality of craft and, judging by their weathering, in age as well.

The crowd thickened and grew more excited as they got closer to the Circus. The noise of the bell-ringers faded, gradually replaced by a new racket of small drums clattering in cacophonous rhythms. Hundreds upon hundreds of Normals and Shallow Ones strode toward a wide archway framed with garlands of black chains, while further hundreds of Digglies and Deep Ones squeezed into smaller gates at either side. Nearly everyone, it seemed, was tapping vigorously upon small, annoyingly loud hand-drums. Just outside the Circus, amid food and drink stands, Aleck saw two buildings facing one another across the street. One bore a huge sign reading GIVER DRUMS; the other, REAL GIVER DRUMS. *What's with all the freakin' noisemakers in this town?*

"How do we get in?" asked Aleck.

"Just sneak past the box office."

"What about you? They allow giant dogs in the stands?"

"Nobody sees me if I don't wanna be seen."

"Seriously?"

"Eh, more or less."

"Like a Keeper robe?"

"Nah, not really. C'mon."

Aleck glowered at Akaz as he loped away, then hustled through the crowd to catch up.

Bas-reliefs covered the outer wall of the Circus, depicting musicians, athletes, and figures that Aleck thought must be actors. He now saw that the chains draped around the main gates, partly obscuring the words CIRCVS OF BRIGHT SKILLS, had hundreds of charred skulls lashed to them, garlands of rust and bone. Shuddering, Aleck snuck past the box office. *These motherfuckers gotta die.*

The torch-lit hallway echoed with the clamor of a hundred aggressive little drums. Aleck kept his fingers tangled in the fur of Akaz's neck, allowing himself to be led through the branching crowd. They went down tunnels, up stairways, and emerged into sunlight, halfway up one side of the arena. The drone of drums and cheering rose and fell like curtains of rain passing across a roof. Four Herax boats circled high overhead while numerous small, rectangular rafts flew slowly around, swooping low over the stands. Several rafts carried small groups of warriors: muscular Normal men, garbed in all manner of clothing and armor, wielding a variety of weaponry. Many of them roared and waved their weapons around, clamoring for attention; others studied the uneven terrain of the arena floor. Displayed on the other rafts, each accompanied by a proud and preening fighter, were the Nubiles, smiling and waving, chained by the neck.

"Why the hell are the Nubiles smiling?" asked Aleck.

"They feed on other people's pleasure," said Akaz, "whatever form that pleasure takes, just like Apraxos feeds on any kind of suffering. I don't know why they were crying when the Herax took them, since I'm sure the Herax were enjoying themselves. Maybe it took them a while to get used to it. Looks like they've acclimated now."

The thought made Aleck sick.

"Gentlemen and underlings!" An enormous voice startled Aleck. It seemed to come from everywhere at once. The crowd surged in response. "Now that we have our first five champions, let us pause before we watch them ravish their Nymphs. For behold: Today we strike a mighty blow against the Givers!"

Aleck recognized the magically amplified voice: Apraxos the Watcher. He looked around. "Where is he?"

"Behind you."

Aleck jumped, a pang of adrenaline coursing into his fingers. He turned and saw gaunt Apraxos directly above and behind him, standing on an elevated balcony, surrounded by Herax guards.

"The Givers preach heresies and raise up false prophets!" screamed Minister Apraxos. The crowd roared like a windstorm. "And who is the falsest of their prophets?"

The crowd chanted. Aleck couldn't make out the phrase they were repeating.

"Yes, Blood Eagle!" said Apraxos. "Blood Eagle, who tried to unify the Givers of Fire and Flame, and failed!" The crowd cheered in agreement. "Blood Eagle, who perverted our sacred prophecy of the Cannibal-King, predicting a false savior that will never arrive! And who has led his forces against us, to no avail: behold!"

A flash and a puff of smoke, and alone on the sandy floor of the arena stood a huge, muscular, hairless man, covered in jagged patterns of red welts. He carried no weapons. A heavy muzzle of black leather hid the bottom half of his face.

The crowd went berserk with shouting and drums, chanting *Blood Eagle! Blood Eagle!* The warriors on the rafts danced with excitement. Aleck saw one of them knocked overboard; he tumbled down through the air and landed on a spectator. Both lay unmoving.

"Holy smokes," said Akaz, "It really is Blood Eagle."

"You *know* that guy?"

"Sure. Now that's what I call auspicious. I told ya you had Weird Luck, kid."

"How do you mean?"

"What's the chances of us just bumping into the Second Herald?" asked Akaz. "Poor guy. It looks like they cut out his brandings."

"They *what?*"

"Check him out, he's covered in spiral wounds. He used to have magical patterns branded all over his body."

"Branded?" Aleck stared down at Blood Eagle. *"Cut out his brandings?"*

"Yeah. Givers like fire. Branding gives them holy powers. Looks like Apraxos cut out his scars to rid him of his magic."

Dumbfounded, Aleck looked back and forth in horror between Akaz and Blood Eagle.

"I bet it didn't work." Akaz snickered. "Bet it backfired."

Apraxos shouted again in his giant voice. "What shall we do with him?"

Aleck stared up at Apraxos, wishing he had somehow brought a gun with him from Earth. Not that he knew how to shoot.

The crowd chanted an unintelligible word over and over.

"What shall we do with him?" repeated Apraxos.

The crowd chanted, and Aleck realized they were shouting *Troll, troll, troll.*

A huge humanoid figure lumbered onto the arena floor. A giant cleaver and long knife hung from its belt; overlapping scales of rusty metal armor jangled with its bow-legged stride. Its gnarled arms swung low, scraping massive fists across the sandy ground. Towering over Blood Eagle, the troll brandished the cleaver over its head and opened its tusked jaws in a trumpeting roar.

"Dude," said Aleck.

"Watch," said Akaz.

Blood Eagle dove in close beside the troll, taking the knife from its belt as he ran past. He spun and chopped open the back of the troll's leg. The troll screamed in surprise and turned around, staggering, falling heavily to one knee. Blood Eagle sliced the troll's wrist, and the cleaver fell from its hand. It roared again. Blood Eagle shoved the knife in its eye to the hilt.

Aleck stared, awestruck. The crowd fell silent. The troll knelt in place, swaying slightly. Blood Eagle pulled the knife from its eye socket and used it to cut the muzzle away from his own face. Then, tossing the knife aside, he hefted the massive cleaver and laid it deep into the troll's throat. The troll toppled over backwards. Blood Eagle hauled the cleaver out of its neck and buried his face in the gaping wound. Silence hung over the Circus. Aleck blinked.

Blood Eagle looked up, gore streaming down his face and over his chest. The angry red wounds covering his body had suddenly healed to pale scars. He snarled, showing rows of pointed teeth.

The crowd burst into a thunderous mix of cheering and booing. Blood Eagle sprinted to the nearest wall of the arena.

"Here we go." Akaz leaned forward.

Blood Eagle heaved himself up at the feet of a Herax soldier. As the Herax raised his spear to strike, Blood Eagle dodged in close and head-butted him in the face. Taking the dazed soldier's spear, he stabbed him under the chin, pitching him down onto the arena floor like a shovelful of dirt. Aleck cheered along with the crowd's mixed roar of cheers and outrage. Blood Eagle ran through the stands, knocking spectators aside with the spear. He came up under one of the flying rafts and used the spear to vault himself up.

On the raft stood a warrior in furs with a hatchet in each hand. Beside him knelt one of the Nubiles. She greeted Blood Eagle with a sultry, amplified "Hello" that resonated through the arena, provoking scattered laughter from the stands.

The warrior bashed her in the face with the butt of a hatchet, knocking her down. "Hey!" Aleck again wished for a gun. She sat up, unharmed and chuckling. "Ick," said Aleck. The crowd laughed again. "Ick."

Enraged, the warrior hurled one of his hatchets at Blood Eagle, who snatched it out of the air and flung it back. The warrior stumbled overboard, hatchet in his face. The raft swung toward Aleck and Akaz on its lazy arc.

"Fuck," said Aleck.

"Do it now!" said Akaz, suddenly.

"What? Huh? Do what?"

"The thing, do the thing! The Token!"

"What?" Then Aleck remembered the *Token of Time Dilation*. "Why don't you do it?"

"Because of his Sovereign Shield!"

"Doesn't that affect me, too?"

"Nowhere near as bad as if I do it!" Smoke and flame billowed from Akaz's eye sockets. "*Hurry!*"

Aleck frowned. He put the enchanted shell into his mouth and tasted the slow ocean. The world around him froze and fell silent. Dizziness overcame him, and he nearly spat out the Token to make it stop; but the Nymph's warning returned to him: this was his one chance. He breathed deeply. The people around him, whom he had thought entirely frozen, shifted almost imperceptibly with smooth, exquisite motion. Low humming surrounded him in the air, but no sound that he could properly identify.

"How do ya feel, kid?"

"Hmmh?" Aleck again almost spat out the Token. Akaz sat beside him, unmoving, his jaws hanging slightly open. His eyes of fire flickered quickly, like normal fire.

"I said, how do you feel?" came Akaz's voice from his unmoving mouth.

Aleck shifted the Token into his cheek. "How can you talk to me?"

"I'm a magic dog." Akaz spoke in a patronizing tone, motionless but for his eyes. "You don't want to use that thing for too long. Go fetch the Circomangkus and get us out of here before you wear yourself out."

"Fetch the *what?*"

"The Circomangkus. That amulet Apraxos is wearing. It controls the magic of the Circus — the rafts, most importantly. Grab that thing and you can fly us out of here. And grab the damn Skull of Kaios while you're at it!"

Aleck's dizziness had passed. He found he kinda liked the taste of the Token after all. He ran up the stair alongside the balcony, past unmoving Herax guards, and hauled himself up onto the wall. A dozen Herax spearmen stood like statues around the perimeter of the balcony. Apraxos leaned out at the wall, fist raised. Aleck saw two broad divans, one of them occupied by an enormous man in a sharp black uniform. Aleck waited on the wall, hands in his pockets. Watching them all slowly turn to look at him, he realized the extent of the power of the Token.

The guard nearest him swung the butt of his spear toward Aleck's legs. Aleck casually stepped over it. He debated with himself for a moment, then punted the Herax in the face. The guard toppled over swiftly, at Aleck's rate of motion, landing with a thump in his spear-swinging pose; then, very slowly, he flattened out upon the floor.

Aleck watched the rest of the guards shift languidly into fighting stances. A heavy spear glided toward him, point-first, aimed expertly at the center of his chest. "Akaz!" he snapped, drooling a little as he spoke around the Token.

"What," said Akaz from below.

Aleck wiped his mouth. "This pig is trying to kill me! All I'm doing is standing on the wall, and he thinks it's okay to just kill me!"

"He's just doing his job. You're trespassing."

That hit a nerve. The Trespassers' Club had almost been caught at times, but never impaled. "What the hell is wrong with this place?"

"It's no different from Earth."

That only made Aleck madder. Clenching his teeth, he

stepped aside, lifted the spear out of the air, and turned it end for end. The Herax stood with his arm outstretched, still following through from his throw, lips parted in a fanged snarl. Livid, Aleck hopped down from the parapet. He notched the tip of the spear between the soldier's teeth.

"Fuck you, pig!" He shoved on the haft with all his might. The Herax fell over backward, the wide spear-point emerging where neck met skull.

Aleck stood there, startled, watching in horror as the soldier's blood flowed slow as honey across the tiled floor. A wave of anxiety and weakness swept through his body. He looked around in a daze.

"Come on," said Akaz. "Get the amulet. Get the Skull."

"Anarchist!" thundered the voice of Apraxos, echoing throughout the arena.

Aleck jumped, nearly spitting out the Token. "What, you too?"

Apraxos stood motionless, his mask facing directly at Aleck. "Herald of evil, you will never leave here alive!"

Deep, heavy laughter emanated from the huge man on the couch, who also stared at Aleck from his frozen, half-risen posture.

"Get the stuff!" came Akaz's voice from below.

Aleck stood, weak-kneed. His body felt fragile. *The Token must be taking its toll upon me.* If he spat it out now, though, he would be killed — or worse. He wondered how it would feel to have his soul eaten.

Apraxos stood immobile, hunched and tensed as though ready to pounce. The Circomangkus, an intricate golden sphere, hung from a long chain around his neck. Spears from all directions floated toward Aleck on the air. Taking a deep breath, he ducked around them and ran directly up to Apraxos. He grabbed ahold of the amulet and whipped the chain, trying to flick it over Apraxos's head. It caught under his hood. The pale mask smirked at him. The uniformed giant laughed on, now nearly sitting up.

"You will never leave here alive!" boomed the amplified voice of Apraxos. With one hand he began gradually reaching toward Aleck, and with the other, for the amulet's chain. Aleck tugged hard, and Apraxos toppled forward. Aleck jumped aside and let him drop. Apraxos shrieked behind his mask as his body rattled to a stop, rigidly perched on toes and fingertips. The sound of the shriek echoed throughout the Circus, but as Aleck extracted the chain from the hood, Apraxos's voice abruptly fell to normal volume. "Before I am finished, you will beg me for the release of death!" he screeched, face-down in his frozen posture, awkwardly propped on arms slowly collapsing.

Shivering with terror and weakness, Aleck hurriedly patted the sorceror's robes. He felt nothing but heavy clothing and skeletal body. "Akaz, I can't find the Skull!"

Apraxos cackled. "I have sent it down to the House of the Watcher, whence you will never retrieve it!"

A rumbling voice came from the man attired in black. "Why don't you kill us, boy, now that you have the chance?" He sat on the edge of his divan, smiling at Aleck.

"Don't!" said Akaz. "Shut up, Goromath! Aleck, if you do anything more to them, it's bound to backfire! Just get the rafts and get us out of here!"

"How can you all speak to me, when you can't even move?" Aleck drooled around the Token. He felt like his knees would soon start to buckle.

General Goromath laughed. Holding the amulet, Aleck closed his eyes and visualized the rafts flying to him. He opened his eyes to see the rafts speeding toward the balcony: like the Herax he had kicked in the face, and like Apraxos when he fell, the rafts moved as fast as Aleck could. Warriors were flung off, to tumble slowly, like falling leaves; Nubiles were dragged through the air by their neck-chains. Blood Eagle stood poised on his raft, leaning forward into the wind.

"No!" said Aleck.

Akaz and Goromath both laughed.

"What?" asked Apraxos, unable to see. He slowly began to turn over. "What are you laughing at?"

"No," Aleck whined through clenched teeth, as he watched the falling warriors gradually descend.

"*That* bit of slapstick I must confess I did not expect." Goromath laughed.

"There goes your tournament," said Akaz.

"I had no attachment to any specific outcome, beyond the general category of 'entertaining bloodshed.'"

"Whatever. Still hoping you end up dead after all this."

Goromath hissed like a giant reptile. "Insolent cur!"

"Yawn," said Akaz.

"What is happening!" said Apraxos. "What has happened?"

"It looks like Blood Eagle is escaping," said Goromath.

"Fool! You must kill him!"

"I shall do my best." Goromath made his first motions toward standing up. "But I fear I am at somewhat of a disadvantage, under the circumstances."

"Hey, wait a minute." Aleck stopped the rafts in midair and sent them back, easily sweeping up all the warriors out of the air, lowering them to the stands, and tipping them gently off into the aisles. He kept Blood Eagle and the Nubiles.

"Such compassion!" Goromath laughed. "Boy, you are a questionable asset to your prophet's military venture. I am now even less frightened of you than I was. Though I am well amused, and offer no complaint. Despite the lessening of the aforementioned bloodshed."

Aleck stomped over to where Goromath sat, stood craning over him, and drooled copiously onto his face.

"Faugh!" said Goromath.

Aleck put his face up to Goromath's and screamed as best he could around the Token without spitting it out, "Fuff you, you goofefteffing faffist fuffing fuff!" He sprayed some.

"Faugh!"

That took the last of Aleck's strength. Shaking with weakness and anxiety, he brought the rafts up to the edge of the balcony and climbed onto an empty one. Looking over the edge, he lowered his raft and scooped Akaz roughly onto it, the frozen wolf tumbling like a toy.

"We will destroy you!" said Apraxos.

"Indeed," said Goromath.

"Fuckin' kill you," said Aleck.

"To the river," said Akaz.

Aleck flew the rafts away toward the river, feeling increasingly nauseated. Flying as low and fast over the water as he dared, he took them, single file, toward the bay. He saw a crow clinging desperately to one of the rafts. "Akaz. Where."

"Feel sick?" Akaz lay on his side, two legs still sticking into the air.

Aleck nodded.

"Just keep going this way. Don't spit out that Token yet. Wait till we're out of sight."

"I don't want to faint. Crash us."

"Don't worry. We're here." The rafts shot out over the bay. "Billycutter's Tunnel. It's just back behind us in the cliff. We walked past it this morning."

Aleck slowed the rafts and pulled them around in a wide circle. Glancing back, he spotted Blood Eagle staring at him. He shivered and focused on the cliff.

"See the demon head?" asked Akaz. "Just fly straight at that."

Aleck recognized the large outcropping, subtly carved into an uncanny face contorted with lamentation.

"'At it'?" croaked Aleck.

"Yeah. It'll move."

Aleck shot one of the empty rafts at it. The stone face looked solid, but the raft flew through it and disappeared. Aleck desperately followed. *Have I lost my mind?* he thought. *My nerves frayed under the influence of the Token?* He sped into the face and through it, bringing the rest of the rafts close behind.

On the other side, he found himself floating in a wide, dimly-lit tunnel. Except for a flat path down the middle of the floor, the living stone all around had been carved in bas-relief. Bodies and faces of all sizes and description erupted from intricate, abstract patterns of waves and webs. Stone of many colors striped the walls, with one thin band of glowing mineral casting its light down the tunnel.

The Nymph stood, frozen, twenty yards away.

Aleck set down the rafts, spat out the Token, and fell to all fours, dry-heaving. Akaz jumped to his feet. The Nymph came running down the tunnel toward them. Aleck rolled over on his side, panting heavily. "Are you well?" The Nymph knelt beside him. She took his hands, but released them with a jolt. She stood up, tears spilling from her eyes. "Killer!"

"We got your Nubiles back," said Akaz. "You're welcome."

Glowering at Akaz, she strode over to the first of the Nubiles, grabbed her metal collar in both hands, and wrenched it open.

"I didn't mean to kill him," said Aleck.

The Nymph spun to face Akaz. "Even him!" She pointed at Aleck. "Even him you corrupt!"

"It was only a Herax," said Akaz.

The Nymph scowled and turned away. She broke the collar off of another of the Nubiles, and another.

"It didn't seem real," said Aleck.

"Frankly, I'm stunned there was as little killing as there was," said Akaz. "The kid even went out of his way to save a bunch of Normal assholes. Rapist gladiator types, your favorite."

Ignoring him, the Nymph removed another collar. Blood Eagle stood between the Nymph and the fifth Nubile. She looked at the blood on his jaws, on his hands. "I killed a Herax," he said.

"And ate his heart, I take it?"

"Nay," said Blood Eagle. "I killed also a Normal, and a Troll of Apraxos; but I ate none of them, for such is my vow."

"Indeed?"

"I drank some trollsblood, for I was wounded. But those beasts, despite their humanoid semblance, have no true souls, as we know."

She shooed him aside, a sour look on her face. He bowed and stepped away. The Nymph twisted off the collar of the last Nubile, then walked up to Akaz and spat in his face. Without another word, she turned and strode away toward the entrance, followed by her Nubiles.

Aleck called after her. "It wasn't Akaz that made me do it, it was the Token! Nothing seemed real. Killing him didn't seem real!"

The Nymph and the Nubiles disappeared.

Akaz did his best to wipe the spit off his face with his paws.

"O Great Akaz," said Blood Eagle, falling to his knees and putting his forehead to the floor. "O Great Akaz, bringer-of-fire." He sat up. "Despite her admittedly transcendent origins, she seems a disrespectful nuisance. Shall I slaughter her for you?"

Akaz crouched, head lowered, looking around at nothing in particular. "Let's go."

"Where are we going?" asked Aleck.

"Down this way is the Well of Apraxos. That will lead us straight to the House of the Watcher."

"And we're going there why?" asked Aleck.

"To get the Skull, stupid."

Aleck looked around. "What do I do with the rest of these rafts?"

"Leave them here," said Akaz.

The Skull of Kaios

Watcher, beware
The First Herald:
Flying on trophy wings,
He tilts your ships sideways.
He smells even what is hidden
From the god of the trackers.

Watcher, beware
The Second Herald:
Swallowing death itself,
He bleeds fire.
He cuts your fingers from you
One by one.

— from "The Song of the Heralds"
by Kaios the Summoner

•

The raft plummeted in total darkness down the Well of Apraxos. Akaz dangled his head over the side. Aleck huddled in the center, feeling better physically but now terrified, listening to Blood Eagle pace fearlessly in a circle around him. The Cook presumably still perched on one corner.

"Move left a bit," said Akaz. "You're drifting near the wall."

Clutching the amulet that controlled the raft's flight, Aleck willed it ten feet leftward.

"A little more."

Aleck slid the raft further across the Well.

"Not so far!" said Akaz. "Back a little!"

Aleck jerked the raft back, and Blood Eagle stumbled. "Careful, boy!" The Giver flicked Aleck hard in the temple with his finger.

"Ow! You can see in pitch dark, why don't you fly this goddamn thing? Here!" Aleck took the amulet from around his neck and flung it at where he thought Blood Eagle stood. The chain jingled as Blood Eagle grabbed the amulet out of the air and threw it back at Aleck, striking him painfully in the chest.

"Aleck!" said Akaz. "Is your head on straight?"

Aleck paused, thought a moment, envisioned the amulet flying away into the darkness — the raft then diving, uncontrolled, to shatter against the wall some unknown distance below. Panic flashed through him.

"I cannot fly the raft," said Blood Eagle, "because I am Pacing the Circle."

"He's generating good luck for us. A heap of which you just used up by throwing that thing, you shit-for-brains."

"Why don't *you* frickin' fly it?"

"Any direct action I take against Apraxos," said Akaz, "will turn into bad luck for us."

"How does that work, again?"

"His False Sovereign Shield protects him on the luck plane as well as the physical realm."

"Sovereign Shield."

"*False* Sovereign Shield," said Blood Eagle. "Only the Cannibal-King wears the true Sovereign Shield."

"The false one is powered by the Rites of Haugermath," said Akaz.

"'Rights of Haugermath.' Isn't that what the Nymph said Fuckface was going to do with the Nubiles?"

"No, that's Augermath. Master of death magic. Haugermath developed luck magic."

"Do not speak those names in my presence." Blood Eagle spat off the edge of the raft. "Not even you, Great Akaz. Please."

"Hmph."

Aleck hung the amulet back around his neck. "Can we at least fly slower? I can't see!"

"Fortune favors the bold," recited both Akaz and Blood Eagle.

"And that's why we're flying to Apraxos's house when the whole Army of the Herax is looking for us."

"Most of them are facing the Givers, in the countryside outside the city," said Akaz. "And the ones looking for us are all up on the surface. This is the last thing Apraxos would expect."

"Because it's batshit!"

"Yes," said Akaz. "Fly the raft."

•

Blood Eagle paced around. Aleck sat quietly, more or less in a trance by now, snapping into anxious awareness at Akaz's occasional course corrections. The Well of Apraxos sank on and on. For a while now it had felt as though the raft no longer plummeted, but hung motionless in the dark, a constant wind howling up around them from below.

Blood Eagle stumbled again. "Careful, boy-cub!"

Aleck covered his head, expecting the Giver to strike at him again. Instead Blood Eagle shouted and sprawled full upon him. Aleck scrambled out from under the massive body and found himself skidding headlong across the deck, screaming. He grabbed wildly for something to stop his inexplicable slide. Nothing. He flew off into the darkness, hollering in terror.

Akaz called after him: "Don't worry."

Aleck shrieked and fell.

He heard Akaz again, still not far away: "Watch out for the wall."

Aleck bashed into the side of the Well, bounced off with the wind knocked out of him. He fell, tumbling.

"Stop the raft," he heard Akaz say, the voice coming from *below* him.

"Stop the raft!" Akaz sounded even further away.

Choking down his fear and confusion, Aleck willed the raft to stop.

"Bring it back up," shouted Akaz faintly from far below.

Aleck couldn't tell if his body was falling or flying. Dizzy, nauseated, he held the amulet in his hand and willed the raft to return to him.

"Careful," came Akaz's voice, not far away at all now. The raft slammed into Aleck. He bounced off and floated in the darkness, wheezing in pain.

"We're at the middle."

"The middle of what?" asked Aleck.

"Halfway through the crust. We're at the Gravity Switch."

"What?"

"Flip the raft over," said Akaz. "Slowly."

"I cannot feel the Earth," said Blood Eagle, edgy consternation in his voice.

Aleck flipped the raft over, slowly, and brought it close. Climbing onto it, he found that he barely stuck to its surface. Any movement caused him to drift up into the air.

"Now go up," said Akaz.

"Back the way we came?" asked Aleck.

"No, no, go down, fool. The same direction we were headed before. 'Up' from how we're facing now."

"I do not understand what is happening," said Blood Eagle through clenched teeth.

"We're at the Gravity Switch," said Akaz. "It's not like Earth physics. Halfway through the world, gravity changes direction. The closer you get to it, the less gravity. That's why you tripped just now, and why the kid flung himself off the raft. A little further down, it'll feel normal again."

"I do not know what you mean by 'gravity,'" said Blood Eagle.

"We're halfway through the planet?" said Aleck. "We couldn't have been going that fast!"

"Halfway through the *crust*," corrected Akaz. "Gravity is normal on the inner surface."

"'Inner surface.'"

"Inner surface."

"The world is hollow," said Aleck.

"What the hell do you think I've been talking about?" said Akaz. "Let's go, dammit."

Aleck lay in the darkness, head spinning, body aching. The raft rose into the depths of the world.

•

A long while later, Aleck spotted a speck of pale light far overhead. It grew steadily. Soon he could clearly see the jagged edges of a cave mouth. The sky beyond looked overcast. Faint light trickled into the Well of Apraxos, revealing the vague, dark forms of Akaz and Blood Eagle. Aleck jumped, startled at the sight of a lump on the corner of the raft, before he realized it must be the Cook, motionless and silent. Aleck looked up at the cloudy sky. "Sky?"

"Slow down," said Akaz. "The House of the Watcher should be right next to the mouth of the Well. I doubt anyone's expecting intruders, but who knows what defenses he's got. And as soon as a Herax spots us, he'll know where we are."

"Huh? Who'll know where we are? Apraxos?"

"Yeah, 'Apraxos the Watcher,' get it? He can see through the eyes of any Herax."

"How the fuck is that?"

"The Herax have a hive mind. Controlled by the Eyes of Kaios. Apraxos and Goromath have the Eyes. Two of them, anyway."

"Hive mind?"

"Telepathic. They made it into a hierarchy. Any Herax can see through the eyes of those below him. Fucked up authoritarian bullshit baked right into the enchantment. Assholes. Anyway, Apraxos and Goromath can see through every one of them."

"Do we have any idea where the Skull is?" asked Aleck.

"In the House of the Watcher somewheres."

"And how are we supposed to find it?"

"Old Aleck got us this." Akaz hawked and spat a human jawbone of golden metal onto the deck of the raft. "We picked it up just before you got here. I figure you can probably use it like a divining rod."

"What?"

"Try it, see if it works."

"What the hell is it?"

"The Jawbone of Zebdod. Zebdod's an evil spirit that Apraxos made from the Skull of Kaios. He's one of the False Skulls. The Astral Web was another."

"I understand everything up to the word 'jawbone,'" said Aleck.

Akaz tapped the Jawbone with his nose. "Look, just do the fuckin' thing."

"What the hell am I supposed to do?"

"Pick it up, and try to find the Skull of Kaios with it."

"This is your plan!?"

"Do the thing."

"And if it doesn't work, then what? We search Apraxos's castle, room by room, until we find it?"

"Well if you have to do it that way, you'll be glad to have Blood Eagle and the Cook to help with any trouble."

"*Me!?*" asked Aleck.

"Just try the damn Jaw. You don't know how magic works. I do."

Exasperated, Aleck picked up the Jawbone of Zebdod and held it in both hands, teeth facing up. "This is goddamn stupid." He took a deep breath and visualized a golden skull.

The jawbone tugged sharply upward, toward the mouth of the Well. Aleck jumped, almost dropping it.

"Whoa, I felt something, hate to admit it." He pointed toward the rim of the Well.

"Told ya," said Akaz.

Aleck furrowed his brow and tried it again. The Jawbone half-chomped upwards.

"That's how magic works. Use the fake jawbone to find the real Skull. It makes sense, if you think about it. They're connected."

"Now what?"

"Hang on to that Jawbone," said Akaz. "I guess maybe just fly up really fast and hope no one sees us on our way past."

"'Fortune favors the bold,'" said Blood Eagle.

"Let's try it. Don't stop until we're about a mile up."

"Are you serious?"

"Dead serious. Do it now. Top speed. Lay flat so you don't fall off."

Reluctantly, Aleck stretched out, and wished the raft upward. It sped faster and faster, the wind beating down until Aleck feared it would peel him from the surface of the raft and fling him into the abyss. Blood Eagle stood beside him, staring up. Then they hurtled out through the mouth of the Well of Apraxos and up into the warm gray sky.

"Slow down," said Akaz after a few moments. "Nobody saw us, I think. Why don't you check that Jawbone again."

The air was hot and thickly humid. Aleck brought the raft to a stop in the mist. Lying flat on his back, holding the Jawbone by its two ends, he envisioned the Skull of Kaios. The Jaw dipped toward his face, presumably indicating the land below. Peeking over the edge of the raft, Aleck's eyes went wide in awe at the creepy vista. A small castle perched on the edge of the bottomless hole: the House of the Watcher. A landscape of poisonous-looking lakes and barren crags stretched a couple of miles around till the mist shrouded everything. If they were inside the Hollow World, Aleck couldn't tell; for all he knew, they were in a huge cavern. "Though that wouldn't explain the gravity switch," he said aloud to himself. *This is fucking wacko.*

He looked up. Through twisting veils of mist, he glimpsed a huge, round mass of darkness in the center of the Hollow World. The black globe pulsed, casting out half-shadowy, half-fleshy tendrils – like the graceful plumes of dense black smoke that arose when Aleck set fire to little green plastic army men – which then coiled and fell back into it. He found the roiling sphere of darkness incomprehensibly beautiful. Aleck felt that he might lose his mind if he looked at it too long.

"The Earth Dragon," said Akaz.

Blood Eagle stretched his arms up toward the dark sphere. "O Black Sun! Iä! Mother of creation! Blessed am I past imagining to have such a Fate as this, to behold you directly with my outer eyes! O Earth Dragon! Iä! Every being I slaughter is for Thee, for *Thee!* May their bodies feed the endless incarnations of your ten thousand young! Iä! Shub-Niggurath!" He lowered his head and stood in silence.

Akaz glanced up at the Earth Dragon, then over the side of the raft. He shuffled his feet a moment. "Okay. Okay. Shall we?"

Blood Eagle looked over at him. "Let's."

•

The raft sped down at the gray castle. They peered over the edge, Aleck lying with the Jawbone in one hand, the Circomangkus in the other. "The Skull is on top of that," he shouted over the wind, pointing to the flat-roofed tower overhanging the edge of the Well. The whole House of the Watcher looked abandoned.

"We just land on the roof, get the Skull, and take off," said Akaz. "Couldn't be easier."

"Fortune favors the bold," Aleck recited listlessly. Blood Eagle chuckled.

Aleck dropped the raft straight down to the roof, landing it in a clutter of detritus. A pedestal squatted in the center; a trapdoor, broken from its hinges, lay beside a stairway spiraling down. As Aleck disembarked, small creatures scurried and slithered away from him. Holding the Jawbone before him and carefully following its tug, he kicked his way through the debris littering the roof.

"Many bones," said Blood Eagle.

"Glad we have the Jawbone," said Akaz. "It would take a long time to sift through this mess."

Aleck broke out of his reverie and realized the roof was covered with brittle, heavily-gnawed bones. He stopped in his tracks, cringing.

"People-bones," said Blood Eagle.

Akaz sniffed. "Digglies and Deep Ones. Very recent. Souls burned out of them."

A chill crept up Aleck's spine. "Can you smell the Skull of Kaios?" He gingerly stepped back the way he came.

Akaz sniffed again. "No, not even this close up. Where are you going?"

Aleck got back onto the raft. "I can't deal with this."

"What does the Jawbone say?"

"I don't get why you can't smell the Skull."

"Apraxos enchanted it a long time ago so I wouldn't be able to find it. It's probably bad luck for me to even try."

"How come I can find it, then?"

"It's hidden from me specifically. Me and the Nymph and a few others who might use it against him. But he never anticipated Aleck of Earth."

"Oh." Aleck looked around. "This is fucked. What did he do, just herd a bunch of people up here and eat their souls?"

"Obviously. What does the damn Jawbone say?" Akaz repeated.

"Fuck this. Fuck that fuckin' jerkoff." Aleck held the Jawbone and concentrated. "Somewhere over by that pedestal," pointing.

"Let's get them and get out of here."

Squeamish, Aleck skimmed the raft a few yards across the roof and set it down beside the pedestal. Spiders, rats, and snakes fled amid the scattered bones.

"Someone's coming," said Akaz.

A clanking came from the stairs. A glowing glass sphere emerged, followed by a humanoid metal body. Inside the sphere floated a severed head.

"It's a fuckin' cyborg," said Aleck.

"Hey," said Akaz, "I know you."

The metal man stood there, stunned.

"Didn't I kill you?" asked Akaz. "A couple hundred years ago."

"I am Blue Thresner the Undying!" His hollow voice resonated from a fluted hole in his chest. Thresner spread his arms wide and then slammed his hands together with a loud clang. Wind blasted across the roof, showering the intruders with bones and live vermin, knocking Aleck off his feet.

"Wha—!" Aleck sprawled painfully, the Jawbone knocked from his hands. "—ow!"

Blood Eagle, bent double against the wind, marched steadily toward Thresner.

"*Back!*" said Thresner. The wind narrowed to a gust directed at Blood Eagle alone, staggering him backward. Blood Eagle ducked and dove flat under the gust, grabbing Thresner by the feet and flipping him onto his back. An ear-splitting shriek emanated from Thresner as he flailed his clanking limbs, trying to get up. Blood Eagle grabbed him by one hand and one foot and flung him off the roof. Thresner's shriek faded gradually as he fell the length of the tower and down into the Well.

Aleck stared at Blood Eagle.

"Let's get out of here," said Akaz.

"Amen." Aleck scrambled around on hands and knees, looking for the Jawbone, and found, instead, the back half of the golden Skull of Kaios. When he touched it, an eerie tingling sensation ran up his arm and through his body. "Akaz!"

"What?"

"Here!" Aleck tossed him the back half of the Skull. Akaz snatched it out of the air and swallowed it. Aleck quickly resumed his search.

"They're coming," said Blood Eagle. Aleck turned and saw the Giver backing quickly away from the edge of the roof. A Herax longboat rose into view, its square, red sail billowing above two dozen armored spearmen.

Akaz leapt through the air and into Blood Eagle's mouth. Blood Eagle staggered backwards and swayed. Aleck stared, unbelieving. Instinctively, he looked around the roof, but Akaz was nowhere to be seen. Blood Eagle looked bigger.

Huge crossbows mounted in the fore and aft of the boat swiveled to fire at Blood Eagle. Their javelins flew directly at him, reversed in midair, curved in their flight back to the circling boat. Tracking their way back to the gunners, the javelins skewered them each through the middle, pinning them to the deck.

"I cannot move!" said one.

"I feel pain!" said the other. "This cannot be! I feel pain!"

"Be silent!" commanded their leader, severed braids and scalps swaying from the crest of his helm. "The enemy wears a False Sovereign Shield! Attack on foot! Do not throw or fire upon him!"

"*We come as one!*" said the Herax in unison.

The boat slammed into the edge of the tower, spilling Herax onto the roof. Aleck watched them leaping easily down, or tumbling gracefully to their feet, spears ready.

The mostly-empty boat pulled away and continued circling around. A crow landed on the rail and turned into the tall, naked Cook. He flung a Herax soldier over the side, grabbing the knife from his belt as he fell. The Cook shoved the knife into the neck of the closest Herax, dove overboard, and flapped away in crow form.

Aleck stared at the Herax trying to pull the knife from its own throat.

Blood Eagle inhaled a huge breath and blasted a gout of white-hot flame across the faces of the two nearest spearmen, charring their heads into hollow sockets. He held onto their spears as they fell. Stepping forward, he spat the last of his lungful into the face of the next Herax. Skin and eyes burned away. The faceless soldier staggered backward, shouting, "I 'eel 'ain! I 'eel 'ain!"

Aleck gagged, retched, and fell to his knees, puking directly onto the Jawbone of Zebdod. *Great,* he thought, through the haze of nausea. *Typical.* He heaved again and, swinging his head to avoid the Jawbone, vomited on his hand instead.

He spat, spat again. "'Weird Luck.' Great." Picking up the Jawbone with his spew-covered hand, he stood up and gave it a violent shake.

"Ah!" exclaimed a Herax, very close. Aleck looked up to see a spearman bearing down upon him, his strike interrupted by a sudden eyeful of vomit.

"What the heck?" Aleck backed away. Something slid out from under his foot, and he sprawled back on the raft. The Herax's spear flew over his shoulder and thudded into the wooden deck. Grabbing his amulet, Aleck flipped the raft upright, catching the soldier's chin with the edge and flinging himself backward onto the roof. Ignoring his new bruises, Aleck shoved the upended raft hard away from him, sweeping the Herax into the Well.

He saw the object he had slipped upon: the face half of the Skull of Kaios. He clung to it and the sticky Jawbone.

Blood Eagle danced wildly across the roof, forcing the Herax to chase him. Leaping onto a spearman, he took a huge bite out of his head — helm, skull, and all. Taking his victim's spear, Blood Eagle spun and hurled it. The spear passed entirely through the shoulder of a Herax soldier and kept sailing, piercing the stomach of the spearman behind him and landing finally in the hip of a third. Aleck saw bodies strewn about; the stench of burnt meat and bones hung everywhere. Blood Eagle picked up two more spears. Holding one by the end like an absurdly long sword, he swung it around in a wide circle — slashing one Herax across the throat, the next across the face, and bashing a third in the side of the head.

"Hold your ground!" The Herax officer lay up against the

parapet with a broken spear haft sticking out of his belly. "We are coming!"

The Cook appeared, wrenched the spear out of him, and plunged it back into his face. Herax soldiers turned and threw. Four spears flew in quick succession. The Cook became a crow in an instant, dodging, but a fifth spear caught him in the wing. He fell.

Blood Eagle stood with a spear in each hand, panting.

A big Herax warship, with two masts and three dozen spearmen, rose up from behind the tower. "We come as one!" chanted every Herax in sight, whole, wounded, or dying.

Aleck tucked the spew-coated Jawbone into his belt and grabbed the Circomangkus. Flinging the raft into the warship's mainsail, he levered the ship over sideways. Some of the Herax upon it grabbed rigging; others fell. Aleck heard the unmistakable echoes of bodies hitting solid ground. He ran to the parapet. No Well of Apraxos here: this side of the tower overlooked craggy rocks and stunted trees. Broken Herax lay squirming. Aleck stood there, staring down at them. "I did that," he whispered.

"Nice job, kid!"

Aleck turned around. Akaz and Blood Eagle stood side by side, both of them bent and panting heavily. Herax stood around them, at the ready. "I'm not a killer."

"News for ya," said Akaz. "Hey, look out!" He leapt back into Blood Eagle's mouth, and Aleck spun around. The Herax warship had torn its sail free of the raft and righted itself, pulling up close enough for soldiers to swing themselves down from the rigging. As Aleck backed away, the nearest Herax fell with a spear in his neck, and the next with a spear through his waist. Aleck turned and ran away, bringing the raft in, passing Blood Eagle as the Giver picked up two more spears.

"Let's get out of here!" Aleck swiped the raft around them in a circle to fend off the encroaching Herax, then brought it up beside him. He and Blood Eagle jumped on. The Herax closed in as the raft sprung into the air, then scattered to their respective vessels. Aleck sped the raft back down into the Well of Apraxos.

Akaz leapt out of Blood Eagle's mouth and sat down heavily. Panting, he growled at Aleck, "What about the rest of the Skull?"

"Here." Aleck held it and the Jawbone out to him.

Akaz gulped down the front half of the Skull, sniffed the Jawbone, and swallowed it as well.

"Where the hell did you go?"

"You saw me. I went in through his mouth. To give him my Sovereign Shield and stuff."

"You do me a great honor, O Akaz." Blood Eagle knelt deeply, bowing his head to the deck of the raft.

"You have a False Sovereign Shield, too?" asked Aleck.

Blood Eagle scowled up at Aleck, slowly got to his feet without breaking eye contact. "Blaspheme at your peril, boy."

Aleck nearly backed off the edge of the raft. "I just thought only the Cannibal-King had a Sovereign Shield."

"The Cannibal-King gets his from me," said Akaz.

"What?"

"Great Akaz speaks the truth, child," said Blood Eagle.

"Let's just get out of here," said Akaz.

The raft plunged into pitch blackness. Aleck brought the raft to a stop. "I can't see."

"Just go. I'll guide ya."

"No way, we need to go *fast!* It's too risky! I want a light, now!"

"I decide what's risky!" said Akaz. "Having a light is risky! Go!"

"No!"

Akaz's eyes flashed bright with flame, casting vague shadows upon the walls of the Well. "That's the best I can do for now."

Aleck lowered the raft as swiftly as he dared.

Akaz lay down with a thump.

"Why are you so tired?"

"I'm bending Fate, you jackass! Haven't you noticed?"

Bright light washed over the raft. Aleck looked up to see both Herax vessels soaring straight at them, shining great lanterns down the Well. Silhouettes of soldiers clung eagerly to the rigging. Aleck dropped the raft faster.

"They're catching up," said Akaz.

Aleck looked up and saw the Herax boat quickly gaining on them, the two-masted ship lagging behind it. Aleck stopped the raft abruptly, knocking himself and Blood Eagle hard to the deck. The Herax boat shot past, cracking its mast across a corner of the raft. The raft flipped upside-down and then right-side-up again, one of its timbers falling away; its three riders clambered to stay aboard as it righted itself. The Herax boat veered and smashed into the wall, Herax soldiers flying loose from the rigging and tumbling down the Well. As they plummeted away, Aleck saw them draw long knives from their belts, and heard them call, in fading unison, "We come as one!"

"And there you go as one," said Akaz.

Aleck laughed.

"Don't laugh. They'll be waiting for us halfway down."

Before these words could fully register, Aleck realized the two-masted ship was directly overhead. Shrieking, he let the raft fall freely. The ship fell with it. Staring upward, Aleck's eyes locked with a those of a Herax, an old sailor standing in the prow, leaning forward against the rail, his face a grimace of intense concentration. Aleck steered the raft with his peripheral vision, unable to take his eyes off the sailor's.

Two great crossbows in the ship's forecastle fired harpoons through the wooden raft. The ship slowed to a stop. The harpoon lines stopped the raft; Aleck swung the raft from side to side, trying to dislodge it, but the lines held fast. Herax soldiers dove down with spears and knives. "We come as one!" Aleck pulled his Keeper robe around him.

"Eat their hearts!" said Akaz.

"I will not!" said Blood Eagle.

Akaz leapt into Blood Eagle's mouth. Blood Eagle staggered as the Herax crowded around him. Like hands belonging to the same body, four Herax feinted in combination; Blood Eagle dodged expertly, but landed in a vulnerable position. The fifth reached in and stabbed his flank. Another set of feints set him up to be stabbed in the other side. The Herax held back for a moment to taunt him.

"You are fast, Blood Eagle!" said one.

"And unpredictable," said another.

"But you cannot outmaneuver—"

"—five sets of eyes—"

"—attached—"

"—to—"

"—one—"

"—mind!"

With that, the Herax moved in again to strike. Blood Eagle disregarded them and jumped straight up. Grabbing a harpoon line, he swung himself onto the ship and hurled himself upon the first Herax he saw. With one hand on his prey's neck, Blood Eagle tore off his breastplate and flung it aside. Other Herax closed in, climbing the rigging or the tilted deck, stabbing and slashing any part of Blood Eagle they could reach. Ignoring them, he wrenched open his victim's ribs and buried his face in the gaping chest cavity.

Aleck saw plumes of fire erupt from the wounds in Blood Eagle's body. "Oh my fuckin'...."

Blood Eagle whirled around and a huge cloud of flame burst forth from his mouth, engulfing the Herax around him and spreading across the deck of the ship. Fire caught in the sails and rigging.

The harpoon lines burned through, allowing the raft to fall away. The five Herax on the raft with Aleck seemed to notice him. They raised their weapons with inquisitive looks on their faces. Aleck dove over the side. As he fell, he willed the raft away from him, up toward the light of the burning ship. He plummeted into darkness. *I hope the raft doesn't hit Blood Eagle,* he thought. A moment later, he heard the raft smash into the ship. He sped the raft back down, flipping it end over end to dislodge any remaining Herax, hoping it would catch up to him.

He fell in darkness. After a time, he saw a pale light approaching from below. Had he somehow turned around, to fall back toward the ship? *No, that doesn't make sense....* Before long he saw Thresner floating in the middle of the Well, standing in the air, arms crossed angrily. The pale blue glow from his glass head revealed a dozen Herax, armed and ready. The wreck of the longboat hovered behind them. Aleck huddled into his robe, praying they didn't notice him.

He fell through the group of Herax and kept going. Before long he slowed, stopped, fell back toward the Gravity Switch and through them again. Soon he came to rest in midair directly among the Herax. He peeked out from under his hood and into the eyes of an angry soldier.

"Oh. Hello."

The Herax snarled, raised his knife, and grabbed Aleck's robe.

The raft flew down, edge-on, and smashed the Herax out of the air.

Someone nodded to Aleck from the shadows. Aleck recognized the Cook, one hand wrapped in a bloody rag, a bloody Herax knife held ready in the other.

A charred Herax body fell past, and another. Aleck looked up and saw the burning Herax ship, far but approaching fast. More burned and mangled Herax bodies fell, some smashing into living Herax or the wreck of the longboat. Aleck swung the raft over his head in time to hear an armored corpse crash onto it.

"To the walls!" said a Herax. The rest echoed in unison: "To the walls!" Aleck watched Blue Thresner and the living Herax attempt with little success to swim through the air, away from the middle of the well, as more charred bodies fell among them.

Aleck peeked up around the edge of the raft to see Blood Eagle, his body wreathed in fire, standing on the prow of the burning, falling ship. Aleck flipped the raft vertical and flattened himself against the wall with it. He heard the roaring conflagration fall past, plowing through bodies and debris. Looking down, he watched the ship slow, stop, and fall back up toward him. He huddled behind the raft, listening to the ship fly past again and finally come to rest in the middle of the Well. He could feel its heat even from behind the raft.

Aleck peered out. The burning wreck rotated in mid-air. Blood Eagle held in each hand a burning Herax heart, dripping boiling blood. "Doom advances upon the Herax! The true Cannibal-King approaches, and his Heralds walk among you!"

The remaining Herax launched themselves off the walls, weapons flashing in the firelight. "We come as one!" they bellowed. Blood Eagle wolfed down one Herax heart, then the other. His body shuddered. Flames spat out of the innumerable wounds covering his body, and an ear-splitting howl erupted from his mouth, echoing up and down the Well.

Aleck heard a metal clang, felt a blast of wind; his ears popped painfully, then he heard nothing. Blood Eagle's howl disappeared and the roaring flames fell silent. The light grew dimmer, the fires on the burning ship quickly dwindling. Aleck realized he felt desperately short of breath. Gulping for air, he found nothing in his lungs. The Herax fell on Blood Eagle in a tangle of mayhem.

Aleck's heart raced. He scratched a tickle in his nose and his finger came back bloody. By the orange light of the ship's smoldering embers he watched the Herax and Blood Eagle stabbing and slashing each other. Thresner hid behind the wreck of the Herax longboat, his glass head glowing in the dimness; he hovered there, rigid, arms outstretched, palms together, a determined look on his withered face.

"Fuck you, cyborg!" Aleck shot the raft across the Well at him. A thunderclap erupted in the Well. Aleck reeled, ears ringing, lungs heaving. Flames roared to life upon the Herax ship. The raft hovered across the Well, the headless metal body of the wind-wizard floating beside it. Aleck stared.

Fresh Herax corpses obscured the view, tumbling slowly through the air, trailing streamers of blood. Aleck watched Blood Eagle leap wildly around the zone of the Gravity Switch, launching himself off of wall, wreck, or body to fly at Herax after Herax, rending with his hands, biting out chunks of flesh and bone, and snatching weapons to use them savagely upon their owners. Now and then the wounded Cook would spring forth from the shadows, swipe open a Herax throat with his stolen knife, and fling himself back into darkness. The Herax soldiers threw themselves after the Giver and the Wilder, always a step behind, their numbers dwindling one by one until Blood Eagle dispatched the last of them.

The burning ship slowly turned in place, orbited by torn and broken bodies. Akaz jumped out of Blood Eagle's mouth and floated across the Well, eyes flashing with flame, smoke billowing from his jaws. Blood Eagle convulsed, then grew still. He lay unmoving in the air, covered with cauterized wounds, eyes rolled back and mouth hanging open.

Akaz looked at Aleck. "Let's go. Grab him. We need to get him to the Corpsewater Nymph."

"I as well." The Cook returned to Crow form and paddled toward Aleck with his one good wing.

Aleck climbed onto the battered raft, swept up his companions, and flew away from the drifting carnage. Akaz sniffed the air. "You're going the wrong way."

"Which way is that?" Aleck seated himself beside the sprawling body of Blood Eagle.

"We're going inward. That's no good."

Aleck begrudgingly halted the raft and dropped it, he hoped for the last time, through the scattered bodies. As he turned the raft over at the Gravity Switch, his face and chest passed through a floating ribbon of blood, splashing him with a stripe of grue. "Great," he said. "Great."

They sped upward in the dark, Akaz's eyes shedding just enough light for Aleck to avoid the walls. Blood Eagle moaned and muttered. The Cook perched on the corner of the raft, staring up.

They raced upward, wind drying Aleck's squinting eyes.

In time, a speck of paler black appeared overhead and expanded into a patch of starry sky. "Almost there." Aleck hastened their ascent. "What next? Corpsewater by way of the *God-Dog?*"

"This timing is bad." Akaz seemed to speak mostly to himself. "Bad. Bad timing."

"What do you mean?"

"I hadn't planned on a goddamn side trip to Corpsewater right before the battle."

"Which battle?" asked Aleck.

"Never mind, we'll make it work." Akaz looked up. "Uh-oh."

Aleck looked toward the mouth of the Well. Moving black shapes blotted out the stars. A faint murmur came from above. "What the hell is up there?"

"Fuck. Get us up into Billycutter's Tunnel. Fast."

The black shapes resolved into silhouettes of Herax longboats. Four descended in formation toward them; behind came four more, and another four behind that, each formation offset from the others and rotating slowly, alternating clockwise and counterclockwise. Behind them came a many-masted ship. The murmur grew until Aleck could distinguish the words echoing down the Well. Hundreds of voices chanted in unison: *We come as one! We come as one!*

"Is this the battle?" The fear Aleck heard in his own voice made him feel all the more frantic.

"Keep going!" said Akaz.

Lanterns blazed to life on the front of each longboat, illuminating the forlorn raft. A victorious shout rained down from the Herax. Aleck saw them, dozens upon dozens, hanging in the rigging, waving their spears and knives.

Aleck pointed toward a patch of darkness on the wall. "Is that the Tunnel?"

"Yeah. Go!"

Aleck sped the raft toward the entrance to Billycutter's Tunnel. The Herax boats dropped faster. For a moment, Aleck thought he would out-race them; but when they saw his goal, they veered to block his way. Aleck stopped the raft, a formation of four longboats silently hovering by the mouth of Billycutter's tunnel. Each moment, more longboats and warships obscured the stars above.

"Now what." Aleck stared in disbelief.

"Not sure," said Akaz.

"You gotta be kidding me." Aleck looked up at the growing crowd of Herax boats, out of ideas.

"We could ram them. Kamikaze style. Take a few of them with us."

"That's it!" Aleck clutched the Circomangkus.

"Just kidding!"

"Hang on." Aleck sped the raft upward, hugging the wall.

"Aleck!" barked Akaz. "*Stop!* Fortune favors the bold, not the suicidal—!"

Aleck flew all the other rafts out of Billycutter's Tunnel, ramming them into the masts and sails of the boats blocking the way. The boats listed wildly, tumbling Herax soldiers down the Well. Aleck spun the empty rafts in place like paddleboat wheels, snapping spars and rigging, tearing away sails, knocking more Herax down the Well. Their magic sails destroyed, the four boats fell end over end past them and down into darkness. Aleck slipped into Billycutter's Tunnel.

"Wow, kid. Outfuckinstanding."

"Will the others be able to follow us?"

"I think those boats are too big. Leave a couple rafts behind, in case."

"What, for them to follow us in?"

"No, leave 'em spinning! Traps! And just a couple. I want

to get as many of these as possible to the Cannibal-King."

Aleck furrowed his brow in concentration. Though he couldn't see most of the rafts, he could sense their location and movement. He stopped the hindmost one, started it spinning in place, then set another orbiting it like a giant fly-swatter. He felt a strange internal sensation of 'letting them go,' and the rafts kept moving without his concentration.

"Even if they can't follow us," asked Aleck, "won't they be waiting for us when we come out?"

"Billycutter's Tunnel is magically hidden. I'm sure they never knew about it until now." Akaz paused. "I guess we'll see if they figured out where the other end is."

Holy Calamity

APPREHENSION ORDER
Suspect(s):
EA00005-23175AMW aka "Alexander Metatron Woad"
EX00023-37618BAW aka "Beth Ali Woad"

Coordinates:
KX00023, aka "Kaios-X00023," 19°59'12" x 27°43'38", 05:17:23 ABS

Warnings:
See Suspects' files. BRIEF ENTIRE TEAM. Of special note are several items (following).
MODERATE: Suspects both affiliated with Order of Eight Directions, ITO (i.e., Interdimensional Terrorist Organization).
EXTREME: Suspects both possess ECSS (i.e., Extreme Chronic Synchronicity Syndrome).
EXTREME: One known possible temporal recursion at apprehension site (i.e., Suspect AMW's for-

mer self).

Recommendation:
One full Interceptor platoon, minimum. All en-
hancements.

Ordered by:
EX00023-08018BZX
Belial Z. Xax, Senior Special Agent

•

Aleck flew them out through the demon head.

Outside Billycutter's Tunnel waited a hundred Herax ships like a swarm of giant, angry bees. Thousands of voices buzzed in the air around them: *We come as one. We come as one.* His mind spinning at the scene, Aleck absently wondered how far up into the sky they could be heard.

"Bad," said Akaz.

Aleck put the Token of Time Dilation into his mouth. A wave of panic swept him up; his heart rattled frighteningly fast. The Token tasted foul and toxic. Clenching his teeth, he flew the rafts as fast as he could toward the *God-Dog*, cutting straight across the pattern of the Spiral Mounds. He landed them under the trees at the edge of the clearing and spat out the Token. Lying curled on the raft, he retched, whining in pain.

"Aleck! You rule, kid! That was awesome. Come on, I need you to fly these rafts into the kitchen."

Aleck looked up at him grimly. Lights from the ground floor of the *God-Dog* dimly lit the clearing. Akaz's firey eyes burned brightly in the night.

"Come on. I'm sure you can fit them in at an angle. Then we'll take you right to Corpsewater, and you'll feel all better. But we need to bring the rafts with us."

"No," whined Aleck. "I can't go through that gate." He dry-heaved a few times, then flopped over on his back. "I can't imagine feeling any sicker than this."

"Then you've got nothing to worry about! C'mon, do it now, before the Herax figure out we're here!"

"Excuse me," came a man's voice.

Akaz jumped, and Aleck looked up in terror. *Caught.* Two robed figures stood beside them among the trees. Aleck reached weakly for the Token. "Don't do that, man," came the voice of the other stranger, a woman's voice. Aleck protested weakly as she took the Token out of his hand. She shrugged off her hood to reveal matted salt-and-pepper braids. She looked exactly like the Nymph of the Shrine, but with deep brown skin instead of blue. Upon reflection, now, Aleck could picture the Nymph's broad nose and full lips — but, with her blue skin, she had never registered to his mind as having African features. This woman, however, was unmistakably Black.

"What the—" said Aleck.

The other stranger crouched down to take the Circo-mangkus. "I'll fly the raft." He pulled back his hood. "I remember how." The man had shaggy white hair, a scruff of white beard, and scars crossing half his agitated countenance.

"You're me," said Aleck.

"Yeah," said Old Aleck. "So be careful, or you'll botch my whole life up. I'll fly you over to the kitchen, man."

"We have the Skull of Kaios."

"I know. I remember. That's why I'm here. It's time for me to do the thing."

"Here." Akaz spat out the halves of the Skull and the Jawbone of Zebdod. Old Aleck gingerly picked up the pieces of the Skull and stared at them, his face ashen.

"What's wrong?" Aleck felt faint. "We almost died getting those!"

"'Those,'" said Old Aleck. "Plural. It's still broken."

"Were we supposed to fix it?"

"Retroactively. Not you. Me and him." He nodded toward Akaz.

"Come on," said Akaz. "We have shit to do. Did you finish your book?"

"Kind of." Old Aleck let the parts of the Skull drop to the ground.

"The book's fine," said the woman who looked like the Nymph. "Come on, baby, pick up the Skull."

"Are you my wife?" Aleck imagined the ridicule of his racist classmates. His integrationist parents, on the other hand, and his White Panther brothers Billy and Mikey, would thrill at the revolutionary implications of him getting with a Black chick. Something about that didn't feel right either, though.

"I'm *his* wife, honey." She pointed her thumb at Old Aleck. "You can call me Beth. And that reminds me: one thing before you go. When you meet a girl you like, just be yourself.

You don't have to try to impress anyone."

Aleck didn't follow. "Huh, what?"

"Beth," said Old Aleck.

"I'm just trying to help you act like less of a dumbass when we meet. And another thing," she turned to Aleck. "Don't worry about whether or not you're going to get in a girl's pants. You will or you won't."

"All right! Stop messing with him!" Old Aleck gripped the Circomangkus in both hands, hoisted Aleck and Blood Eagle's raft into the air. The raft flew across the clearing toward the *God-Dog.*

"Don't make me go through that gate again," moaned Aleck, feeling faint.

•

"First Herald, is that you?"

Aleck tried to orient toward the voice. Was he floating? No, dreaming—

"You look much the same," said the voice. Blood Eagle.

Aleck heard night birds. He wasn't dreaming. He had been sleeping dreamlessly, and the voice was real. He opened his eyes to see Blood Eagle's bald head, engraved with wicked scars, dimly lit by lanterns several yards behind. Aleck lay naked on a rock beside the Corpsewater pool. He sat up. The lanterns hung to either side of the *Death's Door* kitchen door. Aleck felt healthy, even euphoric. "I feel like a million bucks."

"I cannot vouch for the bravery of bucks." Blood Eagle crouched beside him. "You must ask the Cook about those and bears and other wood-beasts. Humbly, though," he spoke softly, "may I suggest perhaps a million is too many, even for you, slaughterer of multitudes."

Aleck gulped.

Blood Eagle spoke loudly: "I would sooner name you for our desert-kin, the trapdoor spider."

Aleck stared at him. "What?"

"I praise you for your tactics, Trapdoor Spider." Blood Eagle stood back up and thumped himself in the chest with his fist. The Circomangkus and Token of Time Dilation dangled around his neck. "And your strategy. In bringing me here, you have bypassed every Herax between us and the Cannibal-King effortlessly. I go now to deliver the Token and rafts to Him."

"'Him' who?"

"The Cannibal-King. I invite you to join us at war when you are able. Thank Great Akaz for me if you see him." He stepped onto a raft. Aleck saw the rest of the rafts standing upended around the clearing, leaning against nothing. Blood Eagle's raft leapt up into the sky; the rest followed, except the battered one they had taken into the Well of Apraxos. It hovered slightly, fell to earth, and toppled over against a tree. Aleck watched Blood Eagle fly away, his ghost-fleet in formation behind him. Aleck closed his eyes and tried to focus his mind. *What the hell is going on. What the hell am I supposed to do now.*

"Greetings," said a voice behind him. Aleck jumped to his feet, bumping his knee. The Cook crouched beside the rock, green braids gray in the dimness. "She had to grow your body to compensate for the Token. Your legs are longer."

"What?" Was Aleck's voice deeper? He looked at his hands. Bigger, older, more weathered. *Why more weathered?* he thought. *Weathered from what, if my body's freshly-grown?* He knelt down on the rock to look into the pool, painfully bumping the same knee. His barely-visible reflection had a shock of white hair. Aleck ran his hands over his face. A scruff of whiskers. His scars felt much less severe. He turned to face the Cook. "How old do I look?" His voice was definitely deeper.

"I'm not the one to ask. I'm no good at guessing mortals' ages. Can't count very high, truth be told."

"What? You don't know how to count?"

The Cook shrugged. "Why bother? Especially something useless like years past." He gestured at the *Sign of Death's Door*. "I picked the habit up from these folk, but I can't count any higher than thirty-seven."

"Thirty-seven?" Aleck laughed involuntarily. "Why thirty-seven?"

The Cook frowned. "I am thirty-seven years old. I recall each cycle of the seasons, and if I think on them one by one, I can count to thirty-seven. But, really, it's a senseless ability. At least something like masturbation serves a purpose. But counting? It's not even fun."

"Counting is fun." Aleck paused to wonder whether that were really true. "Kind of," he continued, unsure.

"Shitting is fun," said the Cook. "Counting is more like holding in shit when you don't have to."

Aleck laughed uncomfortably.

"It may feel good, but it's not necessarily good for you." The Cook knelt beside the pool and repeatedly slapped the surface of the water. "He's awake!" he shouted down at the water. Ripples spread across the pool and softened. No response came.

The Ostler burst out of the kitchen and stumbled down the stairs. "Oh, you're awake!" He grabbed Aleck in a big hug. Looked him in the face, raised an eyebrow. "You look so different. You must be starved, to have grown so much so suddenly." He turned and ran back into the kitchen, announcing, "Everyone! He's awake! And he's hungry!"

Aleck sat down on the rock. He looked around the clearing, then looked at his hands again. "What the hell do I do now?"

"It seems your portion of the prophecy has run its course. Your fate now resumes its mystery, at least for a time."

"Whaddaya mean, 'for a time'?"

"Until you return here as 'Old Aleck.' Perhaps for now you are free to choose. Me, I go to Melkhaios, to fight."

The Nymph of the Shrine burst up out of the pool, splashing them with water. She landed on her feet beside them. "Aleck! You are awake." The scar on her forehead seemed to have reopened into a bloodless gash.

"Hi! You're free of the bay! How'd you get free? What happened to your head?"

"Where is my Token?" snarled the Nymph.

"Uh...."

"Blood Eagle took it to the Cannibal-King," said the Cook.

"Why didn't you stop him!"

"My apologies, Queen of Heaven." The Cook bowed his head. "The true Cannibal-King has arrived in our world. The time to strike is now."

"Villain!" snapped the Nymph. "You cannot stop war with war!"

"When we kill Goromath and Apraxos, our island will be free. I go now to fight alongside my kin." The Cook stood and walked to the kitchen.

"You have forgotten the true meaning of cooking!" The Cook closed the door. The Nymph stared after him.

"The true meaning of cooking?" asked Aleck.

"Cooking is love." The Nymph shouted down at the pool. "How dare you heal that bloodletter!"

Aleck noticed the skull-face of the Corpsewater Nymph floating just below the surface of the water. She stuck her head out of the water. "Which one?" She nodded at Aleck.

The Nymph of the Shrine looked at Aleck, then back at the Corpsewater Nymph. "I tell you, sister, that Giver will sow only seeds of evil."

"The fields of Fate are endlessly planted and reaped," said the Corpsewater Nymph. "You must transcend your fear of death, sister. Death comes even for we who do not age."

"Even you don't understand!" The Nymph of the Shrine sobbed. "Even you." Aleck thought the gash in her forehead had started to bleed, but he realized that clear water was leaking from it at both ends.

"Death means nothing." The Corpsewater Nymph's eerily pliable skullish face bent into a smile. "Sister, do not cry."

The Nymph of the Shrine screamed in frustration, the third eye in her forehead opening wide. She clenched her fists, and blinding yellow light burst forth from her three eyes, momentarily banishing shadows from the clearing. She leapt up into the air and flew out of sight, still screaming, her voice trailing into the distance. Clouds immediately whirled in and blackened the sky; thunder shook from horizon to horizon, and rain poured down in a torrent. Aleck ran toward the kitchen. The Nymph's robe lay folded beside the steps. Beneath it, Aleck found his sneakers, jeans, and t-shirt. He grabbed them and ducked inside.

A mob of Corpsewater cooks cheered him. Soaking wet, clutching his clothes to him, without a word Aleck pushed on the right side of the door and stumbled dizzily down the back steps of the *Sign of the God-Dog.*

The waxing crescent moon hung fat on the horizon, haloed by mist, casting eerie dream-light into the clearing behind the *God-Dog.* A cacophony froze Aleck's blood. Scores of wolves howled up at the night. Innumerable crows hopped in the dark trees of the Spiral Mounds, cawing. He saw naked, painted Wilders everywhere: drumming, smoking pipes, play-fighting with the wolves. He watched Wilders change into wolves, crows, bears, deer... did he see someone change into a tree? Animals changed into humanoid Wilders or other animals. Everyone roamed freely back and forth across the Spiral Ride. Aleck felt electric excitement filling the depth and breadth of the clearing.

He found to his dismay that none of his Earth-clothes fit his new body except for loosely-tied sneakers worn as slippers. He threw on the Nymph's robe. Putting the hood up, he walked among the Wilders and wolves. Some sniffed at him as he passed, some eyed him warily, but most seemed not to notice him. He searched for Akaz and the Cook but spotted neither. Anticipation grew in Aleck's gut and tingled his extremities. Distant howls came on the night-breeze, and around the edges of the crowd more wolves and Wilders arrived, while others departed. The moon's broad curve glowed hazily.

At the far edge of the clearing, Aleck saw Wilders gathering up bows and sheafs of arrows from haphazard piles. Once armed, they disappeared into the trees. Aleck followed, but immediately lost sight of any shapeshifting wild folk. Cutting across the Spiral Mounds, he climbed over wooded ridges dappled in moonlight. Occasionally he glimpsed Wilders moving in the shadows.

Beyond the third ridge he descended to a neighborhood of crumbling stone buildings and twisting dirt streets, partly overgrown with vines and shrubs. He walked past many houses with well-tended vegetable gardens in front, but he saw no one, neither Wilders nor townsfolk. *What the hell happened here? How long was I unconscious in Corpsewater?* Smashed doors hung askew on their hinges. Shutters lay broken in the street beneath gaping, empty windows. Now and then he heard voices wailing in lamentation. He saw bloodstains everywhere — pooled on the street, splashed on walls — but no bodies. Crossing a small plaza, he passed an ornate fountain, filled in with dirt and planted with flowers and vegetables in concentric rows; beyond, another fountain, intact but plain, featured a statue of Goromath spouting water from both hands. A large wolf lay in red water at the statue's feet, bristling with Herax javelins. *So they don't change back to normal form when they die, like a werewolf,* he thought. *Or... what's normal?* Aleck nervously watched the sky.

Behind the Goromath statue stood a wall of fitted rubble ten feet high. It stretched to either side as far as Aleck could see, and atop it ran a catwalk between heavy wooden railings. He smelled smoke. Through a wide arch in the wall he thought he saw firelight dancing on the paving-stones of a courtyard. He passed through and found himself in the New Market. The booths looked abandoned, as did the aisles threading among them. The only sound came from the crackling embers of a crashed Herax ship and a dozen burned booths around it. He thought he saw charred bodies and looked away. Aleck saw numerous columns of smoke elsewhere in the Market rising from other wrecks. Behind the Senate, he noticed the glow of living fire pulsing in the sky.

He made his way through the Market, cowering into his hood and keeping to the shadows. A faraway voice shouted, "Where are you? Where are you?" A cold puddle splashed his ankle and Aleck cursed, then recognized it for a pool of blood. Cringing, he looked around for a body, but found none. He saw many more pools and trails of blood before he reached the Senate building, but no corpses.

Aleck reached the entrance he and Akaz used before. Thick tendrils of smoke curled around the lintel to climb the wall like ivy; through the gaping archway he saw the air inside was chokingly thick with smoke. He backed out and wandered around the side of the building, nervously crossing the river on the stone bridge that hugged the Senate wall. The water below churned furiously.

The sky glowed over the Circus of Burnt Skulls. Aleck snuck down the abandoned street. With no crowd pressing around him, he could take proper notice of this neighborhood. These buildings were larger and in much better shape than those in the slum he'd just passed through. Many extravagant mansions overlooked the street, heavily weathered and aged, each unique, richly ornamented with a technique that made them seem carved from a single huge stone. Smaller buildings clustered between them in bland imitation, each sprouting a monotonous clutter of inelegant fixtures and finials. More splashes and trails of blood decorated this part of the city, but still no bodies.

Aleck approached the Circus. A smoky haze thickened in the air. Distant sounds gradually resolved into innumerable drumbeats, cacophonous shouting, and the throbbing chant of hundreds of Herax voices. Big black crows perched at every street corner, cawing out to one another in their enigmatic counting-code. Occasionally Aleck heard screams or weeping echoing out from the buildings around him.

He passed the burning shell of a small mansion, a broken Herax warship leaning out the roof to hang its stern over the street. A dying bonfire of stacked furniture and Herax corpses smoldered in the front courtyard beside a pair of upside-down longboats. Here, finally, corpses. Aleck hurried past, averting his gaze from the burnt bodies.

He neared the end of the street. Crows crowded the rooftops, croaking into the eastern sky as though barking at the ascending moon. Herax boats and ships swarmed over the Circus like carrion flies on a hot day. Aleck walked past the carcass of a dead dog, its ribs splayed open to reveal a charred, empty husk. A sickening smell of burnt flesh and fur hung around it. Aleck gagged at the stench. Further along lay another exploded dog, with the burnt, broken corpses of several Herax warriors sprawled beside it. Aleck felt his eyes water.

Akaz walked up and nuzzled the dead dog's head. "Good boy. May you come back as a dog."

"Akaz," said Aleck.

Akaz looked up, ears aloft. He sniffed the air in Aleck's direction. "Oh, it's you!" he laughed. "Jesus, you must have really messed yourself up with that Token, kid. I thought you were Old Aleck." He looked closer. "I guess you only look twenty or thirty. It's the white hair that threw me. Old Aleck is more like forty."

"I'm so pissed off at you!" said Aleck.

"Whoa, what?"

"Dragging me into one screwy situation after another, and never telling me what the hell is going on."

"Ah. Okay, sorry."

"And honestly, I'm suspicious of your politics. Your whole angle here."

"Whatever," said Akaz. "Call me a nihilist egoist vanguardist, whaddaya want from me."

"I don't know what that means, but you seem kinda fascist to me."

"I'm no fucking fascist! I'm just heedless! 'Scuse me for being immortal and finding it hard to give a shit about trivialities like the feelings of a naive Nixon-era teenager!"

"Well fuck you!"

"Dig, son. It's over. As good as over, anyways. Still not safe, though, especially this close to the fighting. You should get back to the *God-Dog*. Whoa—" Akaz trotted into the alley nearby. "Come on!" he stage-whispered. Aleck followed, ducking with Akaz into the shadows. Moments later, a Herax long-boat floated past, hovering low like a huge, wheelless wagon.

"I still don't understand what's happening. The city's like a ghost town. Where is everybody?"

"Uh, hiding, I guess. Or ran away."

"I saw blood everywhere, but hardly any bodies."

Akaz did something that must have been a shrug.

"Where's Blood Eagle?"

"He took the Circus!" Akaz couldn't contain his delight. "The Cannibal-King has weapons even beyond what I'd hoped. Those telepathic bastards will retreat to the Herax Zone before long."

Aleck looked toward the Circus. Crashed Herax boats littered the plaza outside the gates, some of them burning brightly. "I want to see what's happening."

"No way." Akaz stepped in front of Aleck. "Bad idea. It's a done deal now, chief, so you need to lay low. If you get messed up, you mess up your future self, and you erase all of this retroactively."

Aleck heard what sounded like a machine gun echoing inside the Circus. "What was that?" He walked briskly past Akaz.

"Nothing." Akaz paced him. "Come on, turn around. Get back to the *God-Dog*."

Aleck heard the unmistakable sound of a large motorcycle engine revving inside the Circus, followed by more gunfire. "Are you kidding me?" Aleck broke into a run. "What's going on? Where did the guns come from?"

Akaz loped alongside him. "The Cannibal-King brought them with him from his Earth. Look, kid, I really don't think you get it. There's nothing for you to see in there. It's over! The *only* thing that could go wrong, at this point, is if you do something stupid! Like wander onto a fucking battlefield!"

"I have the Nymph's robe. Plus, honestly, I don't care what you want, O Great Akaz. I'm not your pawn anymore." He gave Akaz the finger with both hands and ran toward the Circus.

Herax bodies lay spilled from the wrecks in the plaza, many of them horribly contorted and mangled. Aleck tried not to look as he jogged between them. He entered the front gate of the Circus.

"Aleck, don't do this!" Akaz ran beside him, voice echoing in the tunnel. "Get back to the *God-Dog* and wait until the dust settles!"

Inside the Circus, in the middle of the arena floor, several wrecked Herax ships blazed in a tangled pile. Entire trees lay burning among them. Pandemonium surrounded the conflagration: hundreds or perhaps thousands of Givers, Wilders, Digglies, and Deep Ones danced and reveled around the titanic, leaping flames. From overhead rumbled the incessant chant: *We come as one! We come as one!*

Aleck saw Herax boats swoop in low, raining barbed javelins and burning pitch, while the crowd fired back arrows and sling-stones. He saw unharmed archers scrape hot tar from their skins with the heads of arrows and relight the stuff in the fire, laughing as they fired flaming arrows back up. Hooded Keepers shuffled back and forth through the crowd, nursing the wounded with bandages and restorative liquors.

Aleck dodged through the crowd to the fireside. It roared huger and hotter than any he had ever seen, yet he felt no harm to his skin from it. For a moment he stood entranced, hands resting on the rail of a fallen ship, staring into the huge mound of shimmering coals. The tower of flames leapt bright against the cobalt sky. The metal rail felt like the surface of a stove; he turned his hands over and stared at his unharmed fingers and palms. A burly Diggly threw his arm around Aleck's shoulders and guffawed into his face with whiskey-stinking breath: "Akaz Fire-Wolf protecks the faithful, my son, haw haw!"

Aleck saw a pair of Wilders flinging speared corpses onto the fire.

Akaz ran past through the crowd, barking. A laughing Wilder leapt into the air and transformed into a hawk. Aleck watched him soar up toward the circling boats, where many crows, hawks, and owls flew likewise. One by one they dove to the deck of a Herax ship, shifted into wolf form, and wrestled a soldier off the far side, plummeting with him for a span before turning back into a bird. On one ship, Aleck saw two bears rampaging together, swatting Herax overboard. Another warship swarmed with a dozen elk, broad antlers swinging everywhere. Fallen Herax, living and dead, were heaved onto the fire.

Aleck heard rapid gunfire overhead. Looking up, he saw one of the flying rafts he had stolen from here — only hours ago, he realized. It felt like weeks. The raft carried a white Ford cargo van with a ring-mounted machine gun in the roof. The gunner laughed, swinging around to spray a flying boat with bullets. The deck kicked up splinters. Machinegunned Herax sprawled overboard.

The sound of the motorcycle's engine passed by and halted not far from Aleck, idling. A man with a hunting rifle wandered unscathed through the conflagration of flaming timbers, balancing effortlessly as they shifted under his weight. He flung his rifle toward the crowd, and Aleck saw the motorcyclist lean in to catch it: a white woman with long, red hair. Her heavily-freckled face was shaped uncannily like Beth's and the Nymph's.

The man in the fire, just a man the size of a man, hauled a crackling pine-sapling, thirty feet long, out from the midst of the pile. He scanned the boats overhead. Gripping the base of the trunk with both hands, he swung the sapling around in a roaring arc and hurled it a hundred yards through the air. The burning tree turned end for end and smote the mast of a diving longboat, flipping it over. The crew tumbled directly onto the fire, the tangled boat and tree smashing down on them and sending up a huge gout of sparks. The mob in the Circus raised a deafening cheer.

The man hopped down from the fire and got on the motorcycle behind the red-haired woman. "That should give the motherfuckers some strategic data to analyze," Aleck heard him say over the cacophony of crowd and fire. The man looked like Old Aleck, aged maybe thirty or so, but with no scars, brown hair, and a black eyepatch. Aleck pushed his way through the crowd as the motorcycle started to pull away. He dodged between bodies, trying to catch up. "Hey!" The crowd thinned as they got further from the fire, parting for the motorcycle and cheering as it passed. Aleck dove into its wake and broke into a full run, but the motorcycle picked up speed and roared away.

"What the hell!" Aleck stomped his way to a stop and stood there.

"They're us, more or less, from a parallel Earth," said a woman's voice. Aleck turned and found himself face to face with Beth, his supposed future wife, astride a creaky old bicycle. Beside her, Aleck's older self crouched on a pink girl's bike.

"What?" Aleck looked back and forth between them.

"All of us are intertwined with the cosmology of this world," Beth continued.

"There you are!" Akaz ran up to them. "Look," he said to Old Aleck, "help me convince the kid to get the fuck out of here and lay low. He's jeopardizing everything we've done."

"So what!" said Old Aleck.

"What?" Akaz cringed.

"I did all that work, for *this* shit?" Old Aleck flung his hands wide to indicate their entire surroundings. "This is carnage! This is the last thing I wanted to create!"

"You naive, sheltered prick," said Akaz, "what did you expect, a tea party? This is war!"

Old Aleck dismounted his bicycle and let it fall clattering onto its side. "God damn you, Akaz, you said our Cannibal-King would be a 'master of moral restraint'! Those were your exact words!"

"Look, tomorrow I'll argue would've and could'ves with you all damn day. For now, just get your younger self out of here!"

"To hell with you!" Old Aleck turned to Aleck. "Hey kid, do me a favor, go get javelined or something."

"Aleck!" said Beth.

"Sorry." Old Aleck turned to her. "What the fuck are we supposed to do?" He looked around at the crowd and the fire. He asked Aleck. "Do you know what broke the Skull?"

"What?"

"The Skull of Kaios! What broke the Skull of Kaios!"

"I have no idea," said Aleck. "Why?"

"Maybe that's why he's crazy," Old Aleck said to Beth. "It made him crazy when we put the busted Skull in his head. Or maybe we just got the wrong Cannibal-King. The broken Skull led us to the wrong one."

"Or maybe your Guidebook screwed him up," said Akaz. "Or maybe he's exactly the Cannibal-King we wanted! Look around you! Melkhaios is free!"

"*You* look!" Old Aleck pointed. A dozen Shallow Ones hung on hooks, a mob of Deep Ones pelting them with rocks. "Look!" Old Aleck pointed at a packed crowd of a hundred unarmed Normals, surrounded by a mob of Digglies with carved sticks savagely pounding anyone within reach. Normals clambered over each other, shoving and trampling, to get away from the edge of the crowd. "And look at that!" Old Aleck pointed to the fire, where bound and struggling Normals, Shallow Ones, and Herax were unceremoniously flung one after another into the flames. Givers and wolves wandered through the depths of the fire, feasting on the charred dead. "You're nothing but crawling chaos, and this is nothing but a gigantic Rite of Augermath!"

"It's an Autonomous Zone!" said Akaz.

"And you've tricked me into summoning a genocidal maniac!"

"You don't know that," said Beth. "We don't know what went wrong, Aleck."

"Yeah, take it easy," said Akaz.

Old Aleck turned to Aleck. "Look, you need to understand. I've spent my whole life trying to get back here to fix this. I remember this from when I was your age. When I was you. I thought I'd be able to change the course of things, that's why I wrote the Guidebook." He grabbed Aleck by the shoulders. Aleck, stunned by all of this, just let himself be grabbed. His future self continued. "You have to figure out what went wrong, so that when you grow up, when you're me, this won't happen. There has to be a more peaceful solution!"

"Aleck, now *you* stop tampering with him!" said Beth. "Is this conversation exactly how you remember it, from when you were a kid? Because if it isn't, then you have no idea what else you're changing!"

"Yes. Sure it's the same." Old Aleck self-consciously lifted his hands from Aleck's shoulders. "Basically."

"To hell with waiting," said Aleck. "We need to do something right now."

"What?"

"This scene is fucked!" said Aleck. "Those guys are no better than the Herax! They could turn out to be even *worse!*"

"Look," said Akaz, "just let the goddamned dust settle, and clean up details later."

"Shut up. Let's go find that Cannibal-King. Get him to stop those massacres. If he's an honorable revolutionary—"

"You're out of your mind, kid," said Old Aleck, "in more ways than one."

"Is that what you said," Beth asked Old Aleck, "when you were his age? When you were on his end of this conversation?"

"No," groaned Old Aleck. "No, I just agreed to fix it when I grew up. I went off with Akaz, and he helped me get back to Earth. And I found myself back at the wreck of Damon's Camaro."

"Good plan," said Akaz. "good plan. Come on, kid, I'll buy you a beer, then we'll get you back home the way you came."

"You hypocrite," said Aleck. "What happened to 'Fortune favors the bold'? He has guns. He can stop the killing if he wants to, and we can get him to do it."

"There's too much going on in one place, honey," said Beth. "Too many of us overlapping. Too much Weird Luck. The Cannibal-King and his wife are parallel to me and Aleck; add you and Akaz and *their* Akaz, it's just too much. You'll start a Train Wreck."

"Or summon the Reality Patrol," said Old Aleck. "She's right, man. We've been tampering with things, yeah, but not spontaneously! You have to plan it out, and even with the best plan you're still walkin' a tightrope trying to not make any stray waves!"

"Look, kid," said Akaz. "My methods look haphazard to you, but A) you don't know the whole plan, and B) I can see Fate the way you see day and night. You have no concrete basis for judging risk. For me, navigating probability is like driving on a curved road." He looked at Aleck's scars. "Bad analogy, maybe. All I'm saying is, if you go maverick with all these pandimensional motherfuckers around, I'm betting on a goddamn Train Wreck, and I won't have it. You think this is a mess, it's nothing compared to a Train Wreck."

Aleck looked around. Everywhere he saw murder. He heard the motorcycle passing by, at the edge of the arena. "I'm here. It's happening now. I can't just do nothing. I won't. I saw your Cannibal-King, and he looked sane to me. Someone who might listen to reason."

"You don't get it," said Old Aleck. "If you travel back in time like we did, you'll be able to make it so that none of this ever happened. There's no hurry! Write a better Guidebook. Find out what broke the Skull. Summon a peaceful Cannibal-King. Who knows! But jump the gun like this, and he could turn out even worse. He could come here with an H-bomb!"

Aleck crossed his arms and closed his eyes in thought. "But why don't I just go talk to him now, and if it doesn't work, try it your way when I grow up?"

"Because what if he shoots you," said Beth. "Or a boat falls on you. If you don't grow up, you don't get that second chance."

"I wouldn't risk it," said Old Aleck.

"Well then I guess you're not me after all." Aleck grabbed the handlebars of the fallen pink bicycle, swung onto it, jumped down on the far pedal, and sped away. They chased after him, Old Aleck falling behind on foot, Beth trying to catch up on her rickety bicycle.

Akaz kept pace with him. "You're nuts. And you're annoying me. This situation is fucking fine, as far as I'm concerned, and I don't need those hippies complicating it with their ethical handcuffs. Goromath and Apraxos are doomed. Melkhaios is gonna get burned clean of their lousy influence, and we can turn it into a goddamn eternal party like it was intended to be."

Aleck ignored him, pedaling as hard as he could, following the sound of the motorcycle. Overhead he saw a richly decorated Herax ship, flying away toward the Herax Zone.

"Damn it, Aleck, you can't even conceive how much goddamn effort I put into this. I hadn't crossed the Spiral Mounds in years, till you flew us to the *God-Dog* from Billycutter's Tunnel. And I've completely restrained myself from attacking Apraxos directly."

"What about when you jumped into Blood Eagle's mouth?" asked Aleck. The motorcycle headed into a tunnel out of the Circus, following beneath the fancy Herax ship.

"Possession doesn't count!" said Akaz. "Not exactly. The way I played it was indirect. And I only did it under outrageously improbable circumstances, in the Well, which created a Haugermath resonance to cleanse my wyrd of it. Dammit, I haven't killed a Herax in a hundred years! I don't want you wasting all that effort by starting a Train Wreck!"

Aleck rode into a tunnel half-lit by firelight.

"What do you think is gonna happen when all you people from parallel realities, all with Weird Luck, are simultaneously trying to alter the course of history?" Akaz's voice fell to a whisper. "We're surrounded by dominoes, Aleck. Everything we do has side effects."

"And I'm going to prevent some of them. Try and stop me, if you want."

"If I could rip yer fuckin' throat out right now, I would! Unfortunately, that would start a Train Wreck for sure at this point!"

They exited the tunnel. Aleck saw the man with the rifle take aim from the back of the moving motorcycle. He fired at the fancy Herax ship; the motorcycle wobbled slightly from the recoil. Lightning flashed up the mainmast. Something resembling mist peeled away from the sail and dispersed into the air. The ship sank quickly and smashed into the ground, breaking open, rolling onto its side, and skidding into a building. The motorcycle rode up close and the man dismounted, hefting his rifle. The woman followed suit, drawing a pistol from her hip. They both wore sleeveless army shirts, ragged blue jeans, and boots.

"Don't go up there!" said Akaz.

Aleck pedaled fast up the street toward the wreck. He felt a tugging at his foot; glancing down, he saw his shoelace had wound itself in the gears. He braked hard, skidded, and fell over painfully. He disentangled himself from the bike as he rose, kicked off his shoe, and limped up to the wrecked ship. Broken Herax bodies lay strewn across the cobblestones.

Minister Apraxos floated in the air directly above the wreck, his robes flowing.

"Ah, it's our Earth-boy!" said Apraxos.

"Cannibal-King!" said Aleck. The man and woman glanced back at him, the man keeping his rifle trained on Apraxos.

"I'm busy," said the Cannibal-King.

"I need to talk to you!"

"Looks like you have the same dog we do," said the freckled, red-haired white woman with the face of the Nymph. She pointed at Akaz with her chin.

"People are murdering each other in there." Aleck gesticulated at the Circus. "Your revolution is going genocidal!"

"*Our* dog's inside him right now." The woman gestured at the Cannibal-King. "Want to meet him?"

"Uh, don't do that." Akaz backed away.

A wolf's jaws burst forth from the Cannibal-King's mouth, and snarled, "What the hell are *you* doing here?"

"Oh, shit," said Akaz. "What are *you* doing here?"

"You aren't supposed to be here yet!" snapped the Cannibal-King's wolf-jaws. "Get out of here!"

With the Cannibal-King momentarily distracted, Apraxos flew away toward the Herax Zone, robes flapping. The woman fired after him with her pistol. The Cannibal-King's wolf-jaws retracted. He aimed his rifle, lowered it.

"Oh no," said Akaz, "goddamn it, go get him!"

"You have to stop those maniacs in the Circus!" Aleck told the Cannibal-King. "They're eating people!"

"Oh, really?" said the Cannibal-King.

"Yeah, you're the Cannibal-King, aren't you? What the hell did you expect?"

"Dammit!" shouted the Cannibal-King. "I made every goddamn one of them *vow* not to do that!"

Old Aleck and Beth rode up, both unsteadily perched on her bicycle. "Aleck," said Beth, "come on. This is much too risky."

"No no no." Akaz backed further away. "This is bad! Get the hell out of here you jackasses, *now!*"

"Freeze!" blasted an electronically amplified voice. "Reality Patrol!" A dozen soldiers in black riot armor appeared in a circle around them. Most of the squad pointed silvery rifles; some consulted instruments.

"Two temporal recursions," said one of the technicians. "One foreign; one local."

"Two entirely foreign parallel recursions," said another technician, "with a local-slash-mixed trine parallel — correction, that's quincunx — hold on, I'm registering an error...."

"I'm registering an error as well," said a third technician. "It's off my scale; filtering for ECSS.... Oh my God! *They all have Weird Luck!*"

"Hold your fire!" blasted the amplified voice. Then, a burst of static, and "—fire!"

A beam of light flashed into Old Aleck's chest. He fell backwards, knocking down Beth and the bicycle. A wisp of smoke rose from his robe. "Aleck!" screamed Beth.

"Train Wreck!" Akaz flattened himself to the street with his paws over his head.

Doors and windows up and down the street flew open, each revealing a different scene: rooms and streets, woods and beaches, barren wastelands and cities on fire.

Aleck watched the Cannibal-King draw in a huge breath and spit a blazing gout of fire across several Reality Patrolmen. As light-beams flashed and gunfire erupted, Aleck dove through the nearest doorway, slamming the door behind him.

Naked under his Keeper robe, white-haired, scar-faced, and with one shoe, Aleck found himself on the stoop of a ruined shack, hand on the rusty door-latch, gazing through the trees at the wrecked Camaro.

Beside it, on the shoulder, sat an ambulance, the red light atop it turning lazily. Aleck snuck up closer, keeping his hood up. Two paramedics held a stretcher with Mikey on it.

Billy stood beside him, looking unscathed. "Oh man. Oh man."

Mikey reached up to poke Billy in the chest. "I'm fine. Just find Aleck. "

Aleck stepped out of the woods and dropped his hood back.

"Who're you, Fuckface?" asked Billy. The paramedics looked over, and Mikey looked up from the stretcher.

"Che fuckin' Guevara," said Aleck, "who'd ya think?"

Billy and Mikey's eyes went wide.

Aleck shrugged.

— Oakland, Calif.
July 5, 1998 – Dec. 12, 2003